MARI REIZA

Sour Pricks

First published by mari reiza in 2017

Copyright © mari reiza, 2017

All rights reserved. No part of this publication may be reproduced, stored, or transmitted in any form or by any means, electronic, mechanical, photocopying, recording, scanning, or otherwise without written permission from the publisher. It is illegal to copy this book, post it to a website, or distribute it by any other means without permission.

This book was professionally typeset on Reedsy.
Find out more at reedsy.com

Contents

About the Author	i
Kryptonite for breakfast	1
Animalia	22
Bloody Mary	32
In the playground	42
Weekend escape	53
Rico, rico	67
Schools panel	94
Drunk	113
New face	122
Julieta	133
Julio Cortes, southern male	169
MENTAL	182
Luck of the draw	195
Corporate retreat	208
Teacher beggar	219
FEMINISTA	227

About the Author

mari.reiza was born in Madrid in 1973. She has worked as an investment research writer and management consultant for twenty years in London. She studied at Oxford University and lives off Portobello Road with her husband and child. She has also written *Inconceivable Tales* and *Death in Pisa*, collections of short stories; the novellas *Mum, Watch Me Have Fun!* and *STUP*; and the novels *Marmotte's Journey, West bEgg, PHYSICAL, Room 11, Triple Bagger and Caro M.*

She would like to thank pre-readers Bob A. StVil and B. E. G. Bobela and her brilliant editor DeAndra Lupu @reedsy.

mari.reiza is an indie author. If you like her stories, please consider leaving a review on Amazon.

1

Kryptonite for breakfast

8.11am, third Wednesday in May. Passions fester at fast-paced Gigi's on Moscow Road, smell of coffee in the air.

Table at three o'clock.
    He looks at her with mistrust. How many has she bedded since? Fewer than he has. And the problem is they are all in it together. Their parents and before that their parents' parents. Their cousins, their childhood friends, their boarding school chums. Their weekend escape buddies, their uni playmates, now their work partners, their confidantes, even their alter egos… all the same special kind of people mingling from the beginning of time. *Incestuous*, he thinks.
    'How is Claire?' she asks.
    She used to be so pretty, way prettier than Claire. But he feels nothing for her now.
    'Good,' he says, 'what are you having? Here the poached egg with rose harissa and avocado is excellent.'
    He comes here all the time, feels like he has for a century even if he's barely twenty. He knows the dishes by heart. She

stares at his wet hair, from the shower. He looks odd in his strange monogrammed lemon polo and black fingerless nylon stockinettes with Enduro embroidered in red on the side. Did he get here kitesurfing? In this hail? Curiosity pricks at her to know what he's wearing under the table; he was already seated when she arrived. It turns to pure torturous intrigue. But the waitress approaches.

'Soft-boiled eggs and sourdough soldiers,' he gives his order confidently.

'Fit for a little boy,' she giggles flirtatiously for old times' sake. 'I will have the jasmine tea hot smoked salmon.'

'It's delicious,' the waitress tells her.

'An espresso and a rooibos rosehip, am I right?' he adds turning to her.

'I have converted to espresso myself, thanks to James.'

He belches. 'Pardon,' he says.

'A light one, with a bit of almond milk,' she pleads to the waitress, half-embarrassed.

'And bring her a green goddess too,' he adds. The chlorophyll will do her skin a lot of good. He hands the waitress their menus.

Table at twelve o'clock.

The man knows he looks the Hugh Grant type, only a somewhat rougher version. But right now he doesn't care. He's looking at his female ex-colleague a bit too fondly across the table, even if she could be his mother: a Macron-type infatuation, perhaps. Her dark hair, slightly too long and too matte, is lifeless. Skin droops around her lips. But it's the eyes that finish her off; those tired eyes don't want to fight the world anymore.

'What would you like this morning?' The man yearns to call her his lovely but doesn't dare. 'The avocado is best here,' he says to her, then asks for grilled Wiltshire bacon miso mushrooms. 'Changing the beef for smoked salmon,' he advises, and the waitress tries to follow.

Another picky customer, she thinks.

His lovely asks for grilled Wiltshire bacon miso mushrooms too, but changing the beef for sausages.

'Are chipolatas all right?' the waitress asks and she gets a nod then withdraws efficiently; she doesn't want to give difficult customers any opportunity to be even more difficult.

However, they call her back immediately, for a juice.

'A green goddess please,' asks Ms Lovely. 'The vivid green.'

And he settles on coconut water.

Table at nine o'clock.

The lady is precisely late today in her penciled outfit and stilettos, looking way better than your average Chanel model despite her age. She stretches her well-moisturised hand to her scheduled date, a young woman.

A typical INSEAD-er, the lady grumbles to herself. *Ten years later she doesn't have a single successful start-up under her belt and keeps burying her parents' money, her friends' money... Don't these people learn anything?* She sighs. *And she's a girl...*

The lady herself prefers boys; she had hoped to meet Jean Claude, the young woman's partner both in business and in love, himself an INSEAD-er who must understand well his partner's frustrations. *How pathetic*, the lady judges silently. She has filled all the holes ahead of the meeting, prepped herself thoroughly as usual.

The young woman has sat back down after shaking the lady's hand. She is thinking the lady looks like a smart-ass, an old one. An angry woman, too good at her job for over thirty years; it has fucked her up. She has to have something good for her today though. But the young woman also perceives an undercurrent, as if the lady is in a specific bad mood despite her printed smile.

The lady is indeed in a bad mood, her husband having left her last night for good, according to him, for another woman. Why? Because she is meticulous. Rigorous. Selfish. Too clean and never wanted children. He shouted at her, blamed her for being too clean in her vagina. How can that be? Told her she will end up old and alone, breakfasting in silence every morning on a long refectory table. What does that mean? How can one be too clean in their vagina?

The lady sits facing her business date and puts her glasses on, despite having no need to read the menu. But she will read it anyway, she explains to the waiter as if she were doing him a favour, then instructs him to give them two more minutes.

Thank God it is a male waiter, the lady thinks to herself because she hates waitresses in this place. She knows she's having the avocado thingy. 'I always have the avocado here,' she explains to the young woman. She hates this restaurant even if many of her clients rave about it. She cannot think why. She's a Mayfair 'girl' herself and abhors meeting this side of town. It's even worse than Bank. *Worse than the clinical tastelessness of Canary Wharf,* she groans in her head.

The young woman in front of her looks tired. *It's unpardonable at her age,* the lady decides. *And her look is too neutral. She doesn't even look like a female but a geometrical figure.* The lady takes pencil and paper out of her handbag and ticks down her list, like a teacher. So far, she has not been impressed by the young woman. She takes her laptop out next and opens it, then announces to the young woman she's ready to listen.

The waiter interrupts. He's back for their order. Yes, they are ready. The lady fires with the avocado, and a Darjeeling tea. 'Even if it's not on your list,' she says to him. 'Please!'

The young woman confesses she's not a big breakfast person, especially not in a hip place like this. She has been a failing entrepreneur way too long and is totally skint. 'Can't afford it anymore,' she says. 'Me and Jean Claude usually just have cafetière coffee in the morning. But I've come from yoga today,' she explains, 'and my trainer made me exercise in the freezing cold.'

The lady is still not impressed by the young woman but shows her perfect teeth as if smiling. At fifty, the lady is half her client's weight and is surely fitter too. And she came on this freezing morning with no coat, which shows resilience, for British May. *Yes, you need to exercise, my dear,* her smile says, *and light breakfast is good. Also hot Bikram yoga and a macrobiotic diet.*

The young woman eventually goes for an espresso avocado topped with vanilla ice cream, and the lady jumps back in her chair at the mention of such an atrocity, pretending it was a flea on her thigh. 'And a bread basket,' adds the young woman to the waiter. 'Should we share the goddess smoothie too? You should try it,' she urges the lady, 'it's supposed to be amazing for sagging skin.'

The lady definitely doesn't like to be urged, and doesn't like the young woman. It's almost settled. 'Water will be fine, thanks,' she says.

Table at twelve o'clock.
'So, how's it going?' he fires away.
'Good good,' she says.
'You have enough work?' He presses Ms Lovely.
'Enough to keep me busy,' she answers.
'Did you see what Urban 4 Fish did in Holborn?' He's taking something out of his briefcase by his feet.
'Launceston Square,' she whispers. 'The luxury flats?'
He nods but she doesn't want to look at his slides.
'Did he call you for that? He did, right?'
'I got some bits and pieces but not the major work,' she tells him, feeling neither ecstatic nor worried about it. 'I'm mainly trying to work for other people,' she explains.
'And is that working?' he presses her again.
'Yes. I mean, I spend a lot of time generating leads, and the workflow is not as stable. But I can choose my projects and the profit margins are better.' She sighs. 'It's just a bit lonely.'
'We miss you in the office.' He tries to hold her hand and she retires it from the table.
'At least I don't have to work with that jerk,' she admits, hiding her eyes, as their order arrives.
'This is perfect, thank you,' she tells the waitress.

Table at three o'clock.
'So how is your venture going?' she asks. 'It must be weird to work with your mad cousin.' She thinks his attitude is bizarre beyond childish, often sickening, and wants revenge for the green

goddess, which has just landed on their table, a disgusting shade of green. It could be squeezed croquet lawn for all she knows. But she senses she should be careful or he'll soon claim they have nothing more to talk about.

'It's cool,' he says. 'It's moving quickly. We're in talks with Barclays Wealth for sponsorship.'

She shouldn't be surprised. 'Of course, your uncle is a big swinging dick there.' Her murmur spreads like menacing fog over their table.

He grins. He knows nothing about shame. 'This eternal fucking world keeps going round,' he admits with a shrug of the shoulders. She's not surprised men like him become such a threat. 'So are we here to talk about sleepCubes?' he enquires with distancing politeness. He knows they are not.

'I'm up to some exciting stuff myself, if you must know.' She seems contrite rather than excited.

The waitress arrives with her salmon and his eggs, which he dredges in black pepper then attacks with voracity before complaining that they are hard rather than soft-boiled. 'We're still waiting for our coffees,' he says to the waitress, sounding curt despite his smile.

'Good for you,' he turns to her about her 'exciting stuff'. 'You were always too smart to successfully marry and have a life delivering wholesome sprog.'

He's going to make this difficult for her, she thinks. 'Do you want to know what my charity is about?' She swallows a tiny piece of her fish.

'Do you want me to?' Egg yolk dribbles from his mouth, revolting her. He's definitely going to make this difficult for her.

'A literary members club.' She's brave to come out with it, and he wants to explode with laughter.

'Cool,' he says containing himself. Then hacks down and compartmentalises information in his mind. *A members club, a charity? Literary? Clarissa was never a reader.* He was the one full of books. He was the one reading, the literary pilgrim showering any half-decent writer with the kind of ardent devotion which should be reserved for Martin Amis. He was the one living on Nietzsche. Joyce. 'Very cool,' he says to her again, as the waitress arrives with the coffees.

'So,' she adds after a sip of hers.

'So,' he echoes her.

'With your dad in publishing...' She hesitates.

'You mean him owning the biggest publishing house in this country?' he clarifies, amused.

'I wanted to pick your brains about brilliant, devastatingly witty, cheap speakers for our literary evenings.' She has fitted around half a salmon in her mouth after her machine-gunning of words, hoping it will stop her saying more whilst he thinks. She's having to wash it through with her watered-down coffee, and the sweetness of the almond milk mixing with the fish flakes makes the whole experience disgusting.

'Are you asking me for a favour?' He smiles at her struggling face.

She can tell he's crazed with lust, dreaming of her on quicksand, about to yield.

Table at nine o'clock.

'I'm ready now,' the lady says again once the waiter has left.

'You command,' replies the young woman. 'What do you need

to know? Fire away.'

The lady likes when she's trusted, enjoys the flattery, the young woman's acceptance that she's the best one at her job.

'Our company name is Indigo,' the young woman immediately interrupts the lady next, before she can even open her pretty little mouth where Botox has done wonders. 'It was originally Indie Bay,' the young woman continues. 'In like, "Where do indies go for nutrients? Indie Bay!" But it had to go. Still Jean Claude says Indigo is great. Right colour with us being a blue ocean strategy-type company,' the young woman adds.

The lady hates being interrupted and hates the term blue ocean strategy. In fact, she hates most MBA terms and thinks sons and daughters of MBAs are themselves amply hateable people, even if they are increasingly her bread and butter after bankers. There's too many people competing for the bankers' budgets. And bankers usually like their services provided by younger Eastern European or Nordic totties nowadays. There's no class in banking anymore; it's not like the old times when one could trust the butcher to be the butcher, the baker to be the baker, and the candlestick maker to be... well, the candlestick maker. And the banker to be the classy banker. The lady has done well up till now despite the difficult environment but known all along diversification would be a must to ensure her future.

She grabs the young woman's hand. 'You changed the name because they were going to sue (your ass),' she says to her. The lady doesn't say 'your ass' though.

'Sure,' replies the young woman.

The lady wants to make it clear that she knows marketing is the systematic genocide of anything real but it hardly washes with her. And she wants the young woman to know that she's retaking control. Then the breakfast arrives.

(The espresso avocado frappé bucket for the young woman almost makes the lady gag.)

'Tell me about your product,' the lady commands once she's recovered, and she ticks another item on the list with her pencil before she takes a spoonful of her own eggs on avocado. She feels like marching through nothingness as she smiles her trademark smile.

'We have THREE snacks to start with,' says the young woman, picking at a mini croissant buried deep in her bread basket. The sip of her frappé has left her bearded.

Bearded but un-fervent, hardly a determined terrorist, thinks the lady.

'A chia seed pot coated with coconut yoghurt,' the young woman mentions lifting one finger of her croissant-free hand, presumably the first of three fingers to come up.

'The seeds are coated not the pot, right?' the lady clarifies, and the young woman tries to be patient. She has no choice.

'Of course,' she says then continues. 'Acai berries vegan granola painted with almond milk.' Another of the young woman's fingers goes up. 'And Medjool dates glazed in sweet miso,' the young woman vocalises slowly, putting up her third finger. 'All delicious,' she tells the lady reassuringly, 'all highly nutritious,' she adds, and the lady smiles.

'You can't be allergic to them, they are so novel nobody has had time to build allergies,' the young woman feels the need to advise the lady.

'Is that not risky, that they are untested?' the lady enquires, borrowing a menu from the table next to them.

'Not at all,' replies the young woman. 'Jean Claude says there's no risk at all. And the thing is our customers are the busy kind of people, like you and me,' insists the young woman without sounding too convinced. 'And they are health-conscious too. Their snacks are a break, a treat. A nice moment in their day. And they don't mind paying to have the right snack.'

'Is that right?' the lady hums like a killer bee, as she circles three dishes on the borrowed menu with her pencil, under Fruits & Grains; they contain the highly original trinity of nuts mentioned by the young woman a minute ago. She folds the menu page and puts it in her jacket pocket.

The young woman stuffs her mouth with the vanilla ice cream on her frappé and gulps. 'And the packaging...' she states still in monotone, ice cream round her tongue, fearing to dig yet a deeper hole for herself. 'We are using a great print design company from Japan, a bit expensive but they have done an amazing job. The wrapper colours have an indigo base, like Indigo, our name,' the woman clarifies and the lady nods.

I wasn't born yesterday, her nod implies.

'And then each snack wrapper is a bit different,' the young woman continues, 'taking from the natural colour of the actual nuts inside.'

The lady smiles beautifully to the young woman as she explains away, *as if she had come out of a factory with that smile printed on,* the young woman considers. A factory of old hag birthday Barbies you are gifted when you have been a bad girl, ready to rip your head off in your sleep if you don't rip theirs off first. *Her breasts spring out like perfect Barbie breasts too,* the young woman observes about the lady, but bets the lady's husband finds them as hard as bowling globes. They hurt even to look at.

'And where are they exactly mixed, these snacks?' the lady asks, and the young woman sighs.

Table at twelve o'clock.

'Is he still as moody?' She has attacked her chipolatas, munching one hanging from her fork. *She never knew how to eat properly,* he thinks. He still finds her innocence enchanting, even after half a decade of knowing her.

'You bet,' he tells her. 'He called me from New York in the middle of the night last week and grilled me for an hour over the design of the loos in the parking lot for 423 Madison.'

She laughs. He loves her laugh. He loves making her laugh. He has forgotten that his salmon is not fresh enough just by seeing her laugh.

'I was so on edge when I worked for him,' she tells him.

'Yes,' he agrees. 'I live on edge.'

'He breeds psychosis. He's like the Cretan labyrinth, where men didn't know what was upon them but when it came it was perfectly ugly and perfectly real.'

'Have got used to it by now,' he laments. 'But you know he appreciates your work, he really does,' he leans forward to her, over the half-munched corpses on his plate. 'He knows you still have it in you. And he needs you!' he's trying so hard to convince her. 'We were talking yesterday,' he says, 'and he said he may call you for The Spear, in Dubai. You know he got a sole commission for the whole thing!'

Suddenly she's furious, 'You have to stop this, Ben. You have to. You have to.'

The waitress rushes to them. 'Everything fine?'

'Splendid,' he says.

Table at three o'clock.

A well-deserved slap in the face, she knows. Payback humiliation. He has finished his soldiers. 'Not the best sourdough,' he says, staring at her. 'Another round of coffees?' He calls the waitress for the order, and after they stay facing each other in silence. She is forced to crawl like an insect but can't bring herself to feel indignant; perhaps she knows she's personally responsible for his lack of compassion, for his heart growing diseased and dying. Still she holds her breath; he will expect her to fight back. She expects herself to fight back.

'Your sleepCubes company, how does it work?' she finally asks him. sleepCubes – *what a silly name*, she thinks. *At least he has not founded a squatters organisation called SHIT! Squatter Homes In Towers, perhaps.* A relief, she knows, because London is not safe from this kind of comedy.

'There's a sleep epidemic sweeping this nation.' He's still piercing her with his eyes. 'Sleep is the new status symbol. Our mission is to reunite humanity with sleep.' His eyes, don't let hers go. 'If people can't get to beds, we will get beds to them.'

The waitress arrives with the second round of coffees, but as if by magic there appears to be one espresso and one rooibos after all, as he wished for her. 'Did you not like the green goddess?' the waitress looks at her.

'I am allergic to grass, thank you.' She pushes the glass back and feels her rage mount. 'I can't understand how it can work.' She's back to him, referring to his start-up, attacking him with her eyes like bullets. 'You go round with vans full of beds, delivering them to offices? Instead of Barclays bikes,' she pauses, 'you own racks of Barclays beds?' She laughs out loud and he thinks her laugh pitiful. 'And you force office workers to sleep in them? Confiscate their electronic devices? Rent out to them silky eye masks in a range of soft colours, alpaca throws and top-notch noise-cancelling headphones? Do you have a mattress menu too?' She's plainly mocking. 'Your idea is flawed,' she concludes, waving her arms in a grandiose movement, and for a moment she wishes he would fail big. *What a stupid idea*, she thinks. *Coming here today was a stupid idea.* He is still staring at her, full of sorrow.

'Let's not talk about work.' She tries to regain calmness. She knows she has derailed.

'Sure,' he says.

Table at twelve o'clock.

Ben is sheepish. He admits his timing for this whole breakfast has been a bit wrong. She has told him before. She and the boss had a fallout. A big one. 'It was way before you arrived,' she said to him at the time. 'Even if I stay because I have no other option, he does not like me. Nor I him.' Today she tells him again. 'He does not believe in my abilities, and you pushing me in front of him is not going to work. In fact, it makes things worse. And it's embarrassing. I don't want to work for him any more. And I don't want him to think that I do. Don't you get that?' she sounds edgy.

He wanted to please her this morning but has failed. How can she not see that all the mess he is getting himself into is to ensure her return to him! He is even more embarrassed after her telling-off.

'And I don't need you to take care of me. I just don't.' She is almost crying.

He knows she can't forgive their boss, but for what? She never told him the details, only that he was a bastard, proud of his vagina collection. Was she one of them? Did he force himself on her when she was an impressionable apprentice, when she first joined his studio? 'The world went aflame and you can't ignore the past,' she had told him once, vaguely referring to the incident between her and the boss years before. They were a tormented community, she had said of the times before he joined. But the boss had got better, lost his ferocity with age. Still she could not let go sometimes. And Ben himself had not let go either, once he had known. He had become obsessed with dreams of his own boss around beautiful women, all looking like her. She had said to Ben when she departed that she had loved him, but their love had broken at the edges because of his obsession with her past, feeding her contempt and disgust for him, for him not being strong enough to ignore her issues altogether, or to step up for her over their boss. She had called Ben a limp son of a dickhead, told him she had for years built imaginary crucifixes lining both sides of her bed after what her boss had done to her, protection against his winking phallus standing like a proud shining Excalibur in her nightmares. And now he had to dream about their boss's phallus too?

She couldn't take it so she had left their boss and she had left him. She had saved enough to survive on her own by then.

Table at nine o'clock.

The waiter comes to see if everything is fine.

'Perfect,' the lady says, smiling. 'But could you please bring my Darjeeling tea? You failed to do so before.'

'I am not sure it's on the menu,' the waiter hesitates.

'Yes, but you bring it.' The lady then turns to the young woman, 'So where? Please tell me the nuts are mixed in this country or at least in Europe...' The lady is almost pleading, with her smile still on, of course.

'So, the original produce comes from certified farms totally organic and the rest,' the young woman explains and the lady nods. 'And the final product is mixed at a space we rent in India. They do it for us. It's not perfect, also because it costs us a fortune versus having our own plant, but it's temporary. And it is what it is, and life is not perfect. And Jean Claude says it will be fine.'

The lady's tea arrives.

'Do you bed Jean Claude?' The lady is circling her tea with a spoon, not to mix anything but out of habit.

'Excuse me?' The young woman thinks she must have misheard but feels something out of her chest wanting to hurl itself at the lady, yelling to her to stop digging. The lady types some notes on her laptop and ticks a few more items down her little piece of paper with her very sharp pencil; she is clasping the paper between her hands with such force, as if it were a survival manual she couldn't live without.

'Supermarkets, cinemas, gyms... where do you hope these snacks will be available?' the lady asks next. 'Where are your contacts? Who do you know, anybody at Waitrose?'

The young woman feels like the victim of an execution squad. 'We know someone at Tesco from our INSEAD days, a super senior guy. And he's very innovative and really into the organic and sustainable scene, and into the snack market. So I think he's the right person, a real innovation guru.'

The lady hates the word guru. 'I am sure he is,' she says.

'We feel pretty confident,' the young woman adds.

'Is he your contact?' The lady's pencil balances like a judge's hammer.

'Jean Claude's, really,' the young woman confesses.

'Nobody at Waitrose?' insists the lady.

'We know a friend of a friend from Ocado. And another ex-colleague from my BCG days in Sainsbury's, but he may not be in the right department.'

The young woman feels exhausted and starts tapping her feet under the table, drawing the lady's attention to her worn-out pair of Converses. The lady naturally hates sneakers; they say slob to her. She hates women not making an effort, especially business women. She thinks the young woman in front of her needs a boost of energy – perhaps she should get herself some vitamin injections, although she may need Jean Claude's business to take off first, at five hundred a pop.

'Have you talked to these contacts of yours?' the lady digs further.

'Preliminary talks. Preliminary talks but all good talks. They will receive samples as soon as the first nuts arrive on Monday, if all goes well.' The young woman's foot keeps tapping.

'So who will be actively selling the stuff to retailers once you have it? Have you hired good salesmen?' The lady's Darjeeling tea arrived cold and she can't have it; she really wants out now. She has a 10am with a hedge fund manager at Cecconi's and can't wait to escape from this dump.

'No,' the young woman is almost whispering. 'We don't, that's what I wanted to ask you about.'

The lady stretches her smile further than humanly possible as she looks up from her laptop. 'I know a few good ones,' she reassures her client. Although she doubts any of her salesmen candidates would want to touch Indigo with a barge-pole.

'Or we thought we could sell the product ourselves,' the young woman is almost daring to ask whether that would be a realistic idea. 'We are only going for the big supermarkets really, and the list is fairly contained,' she adds. 'Perhaps we can do with one master salesman only, a hyper guru of snacks selling. I could both support him and learn from him. Or her.'

The thought of this deflated, plump, tired-looking young woman on a short leash to a lazy businessman wannabe bastard who clearly decided to stay in bed this morning, selling less-than-exotic nuts packaged in a dodgy plant in India to major UK supermarkets, makes the lady shiver. 'I think someone walked over my grave just now,' she announces. Then decides she will give Indigo ten more minutes of her precious time and let the young woman pay the bill.

Table at three o'clock.

'Any good holidays recently?' Clarissa's whispering.

'Last weekend we had an artists do in a mega mansion on some cliff in Cornwall, invited by these cute band girls who surf.' He smiles. 'There was this cool dude, a vegan chef, and entry was less than three hundred bucks if you had a skill to teach.'

She can't help but wonder what skill Chase brought to that party.

'Dep Farm in Iceland with the lads last half term was awesome too.' He cheers.

Suddenly, recalling what life means alongside Chase, who thinks himself a steaming hot cake from God's belly, she is happy to be with James. *How can a man be so addicted to himself, his own pet to care and fuzz about!*

'Great heli-skiing,' he says.

What does that mean? She doesn't even know. He always did such strange stuff, Chase. The more expensive, the more elitist, the better, as if he got more out of it than Narcissus every time he rediscovered himself.

'Off the copter,' he explains. 'It's too cool. Too cool. And fly-fishing salmon, trout and arctic char,' he adds. 'Evening saunas with vodka fumes...'

She grimaces; the thought of the salmon in her mouth with the almond milk from her coffee suddenly comes back to her and she gags. *He was always insane*, she thinks.

She was always so boring, he thinks. *God bless my days free of obligation...* He is happy with mindless Claire, better than Clarissa. *Does it matter that sex was that good?* They loved each other in their own way but there is nowhere to go now. When something is broken, it's broken.

Table at twelve o'clock.

'Can we have the cheque?' she has asked the waitress.

'I just miss you so much, Julia. I think about you all the time,' Ben tells her. She's putting on her coat and he wants to leave with her.

She has not had a man in her bed for months. She would love to. But instead she asks him, 'How are Isa and the kids?' Then she walks away, her dying hair floating over her back.

Table at nine o'clock.

'So, what about your Chairman?' The lady has started her ten-minute countdown.

'What about it?' The young woman seems lost. 'We don't have one,' she finally admits. Then she feels momentarily embarrassed. 'We are all sort of *consiglieri* to our own board. This is how myself and JC, I mean Jean Claude, see each other at the moment. This is the kind of company Indigo is.'

'*Consiglieri*...' the lady repeats in a perfect Italian accent. 'Is that not from The Godfather?'

'JC and I agreed this structure would be the best, for now,' the young woman explains.

'And where is Jean Claude today?' The lady needs to scratch her itch, feed her curiosity. She needs acknowledgement that her intuition is spot on.

'He apologises he could not make it,' reveals the woman.

He's definitely in bed. The lady is sure JC is a lazy bastard like her soon-to-be ex-husband, and possibly a cheat too. And he's definitely in bed. *Five minutes to go,* she thinks. 'Should we ask for the bill?'

Table at three o'clock.

'I'll get the bill.' Chase makes a move to the waitress, offering her his credit card. The waitress is new, he realises only now. She's cute. He makes a mental note to ask for her number, perhaps tomorrow if he comes back for brunch. 'So cool, really cool what you are doing with the literary club,' he tells Clarissa as she's putting her coat on. 'I wish you luck,' he says.

'Me too,' she says, 'with sleepCubes.'

A drowsy incoherent goodbye.

He suddenly has a cruel sense of something done wrong, too hastily, invading him like a fierce pain. 'How beautiful you were!' he talks as she's walking out, his eyes fixed on a fresh imprint of her shoe on the floor's dust by the legs of his chair. He has bent to recover the alpaca jumper she had once given him, which has just fallen from his lap; they always had a thing for alpaca, both of them, and he has been overly-attached to the garment since she left him, in a manner which could be considered almost Freudian. It was school; all of them had liaisons, brief encounters and never called them relations, never thought they could be everlasting. But he still wears her alpaca even if it has a big hole under one arm, undeniable proof that Clarissa still stirs plenty of blood in his aristocratic groin. *What a pain!*

Table at nine o'clock.

The waiter brings the bill. The lady stares at the young woman until she takes her card out.

The waiter leaves and comes back with a machine. He taps the young woman's card on it. 'All done,' he says. 'I hope you enjoyed it,' he says to them both.

'Very much, despite the tea.' The lady smiles.

The young woman pouts as the waiter walks away.

'Well,' the lady has got up, 'I think I have everything I need. Very nice to meet you. And give my regards to Jean Claude.' She walks away in her pencil skirt and stilettos.

The young woman remains at the table for a few minutes, all fraying fabric. She's shredding her visionary work to pieces, her face dark like a mineshaft.

2

Animalia

It was hot despite having all windows open. The washing machine had stopped working and I had no money to call the plumber. I had not yet met the cheap Bulgarian plumber weighing over two hundred pounds who looked like a menacing iceberg but was as sweet as a kitten. He could have come with his red relic and the false parking permit, and charged me less than two tenners, VAT included according to him, to sort everything out using second-hand pieces from a previous job. But I hadn't met this beautiful son of God yet, so I dragged the washing machine myself, sufficiently far out from the kitchen wall to inspect its back. It was dark enough in there to require a torch.

By the time I returned with a torch, ready to enter the narrow gap I had created underneath the kitchen worktop, between the back wall and the appliance, a bumble bee had got in before me. What had she been hoping to find, mouldy lichens?

I was not one for insects, never have been. And the zumm of this bee drove me mad in seconds. I was sweating, my little kitchen acting as a kind of sun trap which was particularly unwelcome on this hot day. *Why did the washing machine have to break down today of all days?* I thought and sweated even more. I needed something to kill the bee before I could fix the machine.

I left the kitchen for a stick and came back with a screwdriver; perhaps I could kill the beast with the screwdriver's head.

Drenched in sweat, I slid myself into the hole behind the washing machine, panicking that my body was blocking the only exit for the bee and it would come and sting me. I had to be strong. 'Nerves of steel,' I told myself, even if my arms were trembling. I thought of *Psycho*, the movie, and I attacked. I repeatedly punched the fetid air in that tiny enclosure, which smelled humid, almost rotten, but I couldn't centre the bee. Until I did gift the pest a good thump the minute it settled tired on the floor. Silencing the beast provided me with instant relief.

But I had claimed victory too soon and the zumm started again. The bee was on the floor, defenceless, unable to move but circling around an imaginary axis as if it had been pinned to the floor by one of its wings. The zumm was driving me crazier than before. I needed to kill the monster, to finish it off, yet I was frozen. Suddenly, I was thinking of all the Buddhist monks of this world, and their 'first do no harm' teachings not to disturb nature. I was thinking too of all the films where a kid goes looney, and it had all started with him killing an ant when he was little. Or burning a baby fish alive. I had to murder a defenceless bee, and I felt terrible.

Crazed as I was becoming, my heart overbeating and my glands sweating rivers, I took the screwdriver by its tail with two hands and struck at the bee one, two three times with its head. But the more I hit, the louder the zumm seemed to get. And it seemed to me the louder the zumm, the bigger the bee was becoming. Until in my head this bloody bee that refused to die was a huge Michelin bee ten times my size; it was going to kill me. It was going to sting me on the face with its huge stinger and kill me, leave its venom bucket attached to my skin so the toxins could seep and mix fatally with my blood, making me perish. And all for a bloody washing machine. I hammered and hammered, albeit with a screwdriver, and hit for my life, and when I stopped hitting I realised the zumm had gone.

I put the washing machine back against the wall, closing the gap without inspecting it, burying the bee, that life-carrying vessel that was carrying no life any more. Then I started crying.

A week later.

I came back from Sainsbury's, excited I had saved enough for strawberries. These had to be good strawberries; they came from Colombia. I took out the packaging on the kitchen tabletop. I had recovered from the washing machine incident and hardly spared a thought for the buried bee, beneath the kitchen worktop, behind the washing machine. I had assassinated it for nothing seven days before. The machine was still not working.

The phone rang in the living room and I ran to get the call. When I came back to the kitchen I saw it. It was definitely a spider. Hairy.

I have never been one for insects but spiders are the worst. In fact, I have been clinically diagnosed with arachnophobia. The doctor, assuming he was really a doctor, said it was so severe, I would die one day at the sight of a spider. He gave me some lucky stones, but at that moment when I saw the hairy spider, like a devil's vision by the strawberries on my kitchen worktop, I could not recall where the stones were.

I started sweating.

It was still hot; as hot or even hotter than the week before during the incident with the bee and the washing machine. It bandana. It had some Japanese writing on it. In the absence of the lucky stones, it made me feel calmer. And I thought a ninja look may help in scaring the spider away; shouting 'preparedness' seems to put most people off, though not all people sadly, and I had no clue if it worked on spiders. I only hoped the beast would understand who was boss.

But it came from Colombia, bloody hell! Was that not full of gang lords who cut out the tongues of their victims? Who cut out the breasts of their women after they had raped them? This could be the motherfucking spider of all times and I had to be truly prepared. I had to confront my own fear. I had to master it and come out ahead. This was a life or death situation; without the spider gone I could not eat or sleep and I would surely die, be found in a few days by a neighbour, my young body putrid, decaying skin mixing with the cheap fragrance of my recently washed sheets.

'I need a saucepan.'

But saucepans were in the kitchen, which was a no-go zone until I was properly armed. A bowl would do if I attached a makeshift handle. I emptied my jewellery bowl and made a handle with my selfie stick. I would trap the spider and then what?

I would hoover it.

I took the spider by surprise. It saw a dome fall on it from the sky. Perhaps it thought it was an UFO.

Why on earth had I chosen a transparent bowl?

Now I could see the spider in motion, manically trying to escape. It was pushing with its whole body violently against the was possibly the longest spell of hot weather ever enjoyed in British recorded history. Or something like that. The eyes, or whatever I was convinced were the eyes, of the spider, had taken me hostage. Once I freed myself back to life, I ran away to my bedroom. I jumped on my bed and sat hugging my knees, trembling. I knew what terrified felt like. And I knew I couldn't repeat another *Psycho* scene like with the bee.

For a minute, I thought about whether the spider had been sent to me from Colombia as retribution for the butchered bee. Because I know God can work in many ways. I pleaded with him to send the spider away. But when I got the courage to tippy-toe my way down the corridor to the kitchen door and gently put half my face through the doorframe like in the spy movies, the spider was still there. And it had moved! It was alive.

I ran back to the bed, to the knee-hugging position. Could spiders climb beds? Could large, hairy, Colombian spiders climb beds? My mobile was in my shorts pocket. I needed help. Despite being a feminist. Anyone in their right mind would agree the situation required a man. I called my boyfriend at work.

He laughed.

I told him he had to come, that the size and hairiness of the spider demanded it.

He laughed again.

I told him I could die, that I couldn't find my lucky stones.

He said he had a lot to do. Something about someone just below him in the chain of command gunning for his job.

I told him I would split up with him if he didn't do the honourable thing.

He hung up.

Option two. I would have to fight on my own.

I reached to the drawer of my bedside table and pulled out a bowl and my heart was pounding with every thump. The brute was a fighter, looked more of a ninja than I did. It was definitely fixing me with its eyes across the bowl telling me once it got out it would finish me off. And I was sweating again all over my bandana, tension flowing from my left to my right eye socket and back faster and faster.

I ran for the hoover.

I would need to slightly lift the bowl. There was no other way. Hoovering across the bowl was a physical impossibility. What if the devilish beast escaped before it was hoovered? What if the hoover was not powerful enough? What if the hellish creature tried to flee after being hoovered? Would it die inside the hoover? In the hoover bag, buried in dust and entangled in hair? Too many questions. It was one for Google. I prayed for it to give me findings quickly and skipped the data... According to Google, anything over 220 air watts would be fine, so I went for it, even if my nature abhors the vacuum.

A week later.

I still had not had a single good night of sleep, worried about the spider walking out of my hoover, even if I had consigned the appliance to my terrace and kept the terrace doors firmly locked at all times despite the heat in the flat. I admitted having used the wrong strategy the week before; how I wished I had instead waved the spider down the toilet. Because I kept seeing its ghost everywhere. Over that same spot it had first been on the kitchen worktop. In the bath as I showered. Even on my food. My boyfriend, who I insisted carry out a thorough search of the apartment that same day once he made it home, said

I was being irrational. Needless to say I had never touched those strawberries that had costed me my savings; they had gone straight in the bin.

I was knackered, in a long cotton t-shirt, holding a cup of tea between my hands, gazing to the horizon through the closed door of my terrace, trying to impersonate Kim Basinger in *9 1/2 Weeks* although I looked nothing like her. And that was when I saw it. It was a pigeon's corpse. It was on my terrace tiles, pretty much at the centre, to the right of the reclining chair.

Had this pigeon been attacked by a fox? A cat? A big rat? I lived on the third floor, the terrace surrounded by nothing but air! I had to stop my logic thread immediately so as not to be paralysed by fear. And why did the attacker have to leave its prey's flesh and bones all over my *Porcelanosa* for an anatomy lesson? Had it been God's will? Again?

Now, I am not one for insects but I also hate birds, and especially pigeons. I had an immediate urge to vomit at the corpse. But I had not had much to eat in the past few days, understandably, and only managed some bile in my tea cup. Yuk!

I knew what I had to do next though. I would grab a plastic bag, run in and out of the terrace with the pigeon corpse in the bag and feed it to the bins downstairs. Even if the spider was free out there, watching me, having escaped from the hoover, I would give it no time for revenge. Not if I was fast enough. I had been diligent with my athletics training despite all the recent upsets; I would be as quick as Speedy Gonzales.

Except when I returned from the kitchen to the living room ready for the operation, having put gloves and shoes on, grabbed the refuse bag and disposed of my tea cum bile down the kitchen drain, I could not believe what I was seeing. It was truly the scene of a horror movie. It was not *Psycho* but *The Birds*. Daddy or Lover or Brother pigeon, whoever it was, was trying to lift Corpse pigeon to carry it to a safe place.

'It's dead, mate. It's dead!' I cried before letting myself fall back on my sofa in despair. Why were these things happening to me?

I was soon kind of enamoured by the scene though, by the loyalty of the live pigeon who was determined to lift its beloved, dead pigeon, applying superhuman efforts of a magnitude seldom on display in our society. And I stayed sat on the sofa until I saw the two of them flying together into the sunset. Instead of the white dove of peace with a twig in its beak, it was the germy, half-plucked, one-eyed pigeon burdened with a cadaver hanging from his disintegrating mandible.

After a few minutes of total numbness, I called my boyfriend to tell him what I had seen. I was still gripping the refuse bag. My heart was thumping. I suffered a sudden blurring of vision that I suspected was psychosomatic. I was sweating. It was hot. The usual. The nightmare never seemed to finish.

'You are lying,' he told me when I explained.

Then he said we needed a holiday.

Then he said he was busy and hung up.

A week later.

My boyfriend took me punting in Oxford at the long weekend, to relax. He was an ex-student so we didn't need to queue for the punt, and he knew the motions. It was still a hot day, keeping the weather record alive. The canals amongst the meadows were beautiful. We had stopped at a deli in Little Clarendon Street before our trip and he had fetched a great picnic: egg and cress sandwiches, sausage pies, cheese, onion and potato pasties, green garden salad, Victoria sponge and lots of Pimm's.

'I love the reeds,' I told him from the punt.

He smiled.

'Not as much as your muscles.'

He smiled again. 'Let's have food first!'

He parked the punt somewhere very private, where the grass was high, and tied it to the riverbank. Next, the picnic gave us strength then the Pimm's made us soft. The blanket was comfy enough. The shoes came off and then the rest. I had not had an orgasm since the death of the bee and was ready to shout far down the river. But midway we heard a bark.

I was on top. We both looked to the bark at the same time. The dog's teeth were bordered by black gums. The beast looked mean and was salivating. My boyfriend threw me aside and immediately put his trousers back on.

Now, I am not one for insects and I also hate birds. But I do like dogs. Although I didn't like this dog. And I soon saw behind it, a dog brother coming.

'Bloody hell!' I cried.

Was this retribution for the bee and the spider and the pigeon and where the fuck would it end! Animals were becoming a major challenge. No. They were becoming the chief burden of my existence; I seemed to have gained some kind of permanent pariah status as fair animal game, prey, up-for-grabs target, which would terminate me. *My boyfriend has rushed to the boat to get the punting pole,* I reassured myself. But no, he was leaving. He was leaving me there!

And I was so furious, so enraged that I jumped at the dogs, my best crazy knickers back on, and they retreated. They had heard their owners whistle somewhere amongst the reeds, making them withdraw in a flash before I fell face down in the mud.

After cleaning myself in the river and re-dressing, I asked a punt full of students to get me out of there to the nearest city pub where, mother of all coincidences, I saw the dogs and their owner drinking with his friends, laughing over a pint at how his dogs had scared some love doves to death.

Within an hour, my boyfriend had texted me to apologise and check if I was fine. He asked me to meet him back at the car but I ignored him. He texted me again and said he knew a great restaurant nearby which served a superb lobster. I declined...

It would probably jump off of its plate and eat me.

3

Bloody Mary

Young Mary was still reading old Mary's email that morning when she buzzed.

'Mary,' she called to young Mary. 'When are your builders coming to clean my garden?' She sounded polite enough. 'I'm sixty on Sunday and have planned a big party,' she added. 'I need help. I need help, Mary!' she insisted.

That morning's email, which had been the sixth long, disjointed, illogical monologue old Mary had sent young Mary in the last three days, starting from the minute she had seen builders up in young Mary's terrace, had opened with a reference to fallen debris covering her garden, and ended with blaming young Mary's builders for trying to kill her by causing a full-fledged flood on the first day she should have been enjoying a perfect garden Bloody Mary. Old Mary had just come back from a camp in Senegal, and since then it had been a matter of 'Keep on going and duck everything!' for young Mary.

Young Mary muted the buzzer, looked to the two young resilient builders hard at work in her flat, and sighed. The gorgeous one had minutes before cut his finger chopping down a window frame, and immediately ripped off the sleeve of his T-shirt into a makeshift bandage, not to drip blood all over her kitchen floor. She had run to his muscles offering a bottle of antiseptic and a proper dressing, but he had insisted some whisky would be fine.

'I'm not gonna drinkin',' he had said in his own brand of English.

'Just pour it over.' She only had single malt.

'That's too good for it, ma'am.'

She had frowned. She hated being called ma'am, it sounded old to her. She had fixed her eyes on his utility belt and momentarily questioned whether all her orifices would be enough to sustain an affair with him, as if she had forever yearned to be fucked by a non-genius.

'They will come a bit later on, Mary,' young Mary said, unmuting the buzzer. Next she hung up and started unpacking the croissants for her builders, then offered a round of coffees. They had a hard day ahead.

'No worries, ma'am. I go down and take Milen,' said Kostadin after the coffees.

This man was a saviour, young Mary thought. An angel, a source of happiness and reminder of pain in the shape of good things partially denied to her. He had even got rid of the eggs from the pigeons who had nested on her terrace, her previous British builder having refused, coming out with claims that he was an animal lover, he had a dog, animals were often better than humans and she should think twice before harming a pigeon. Young Mary had stopped offering him coffees after his litany and pushed him to complete the work he had started as soon as possible, then never hired him again. To think that she had even let that ignorant man sip from one of her most precious wedding presents once he had mistakenly used it for a drink of water, oblivious to Italian crystal costing over two hundred pounds a piece! It was so difficult to get good, helpful, reliable builders, which made young Mary love Kostadin all the more.

Young Mary waved to Kostadin and Milen to go down to old Mary, then stopped them herself. 'You'll need your own brush and dustpan,' she told them. She offered the worn red ones she had been using for the outside. 'She won't lend you hers,' she explained to the builders, embarrassed. Old Mary had clearly specified that in her email.

She saw the men go down, smiling.

It definitely hadn't been Kostadin's day, she thought. With the cut to his finger and old Mary's madness... He kept getting emergency calls following the downpour the night before too, clients pleading for him to come sort their leaks out. 'So many leaks in the UK, very poor workmanship,' he had told young Mary.

And Kostadin's morning drive to her house had apparently been eventful, according to him. A young homeless man, 'drunk like a fish', Kostadin had said, had thrown himself against his car. Kostadin had skidded artfully but the car coming from the opposite direction had failed to avoid the man, and he had had to help the other driver take the vagrant out from under his undercarriage and left them to call 999, not to be late for her, he claimed, to flatter her. Young Mary didn't always believe Kostadin's stories but liked them. He brought a ray of sunshine into her house.

After about fifteen minutes, young Mary reached over her terrace wall to look straight down to old Mary's garden where she could overhear voices. Only one voice, really, that strident shriek from moaning old Mary.

Young Mary saw Kostadin folded over his stomach, collecting leaves from the gulley in old Mary's garden, at the bottom of the building's downpipe discharging rainwater from the roofs. He was inserting his hands, including his cut hand, deep in the murky waters. They were coming out full of mud and leaves amongst other unidentifiable bits he was placing in a fold of his torn, bloodied T-shirt, with its flattering clerical collar still pristine.

Young Mary stretched herself up for a second until an afterthought made her hunch herself back down over the terrace wall. And when young Mary looked at Kostadin again, she realised there was something wrong. *Why is he collecting the shit from the gulley in his T-shirt?* she asked herself. She understood how Kostadin often did things for show – precisely like ripping off his top in front of her to bandage his hand earlier that morning – but why would he want to show off in front of old Mary? She was ancient!

Young Mary then noticed Milen standing immobile besides Kostadin, holding the red brush and dustpan she had given them, whilst awaiting Kostadin's instructions with his jaw locked, until he started talking to Kostadin in Bulgarian, sounding unhappy, whilst old Mary kept wailing at them with detention-room nonchalance.

And it was something old Mary said that unexpectedly got young Mary to harden, as if rage had made it into her bloodstream and was working like one of those hardening liquids: old Mary was denying Kostadin a plastic bag to keep the garbage from the gulley. She was shouting at Kostadin and Milen because they had not brought their own plastic bags!

'For the love of God!' young Mary said to herself. 'Enough is enough.' And she rushed out of her flat, down the building stairs, past the young Asian girl in number three who was coming back from walking her vanity dog, out the front door of the building, down old Mary's stairs, through the door to old Mary's flat, which had been left open, straight past her grubby living room where dust prickled thickly – was she really going to throw a party in there tomorrow? The place looked nothing like near-ready! – into old Mary's garden. There, young Mary stopped in her tracks.

'What's going on?' she said.

Old Mary froze mid-wail.

Young Mary realised that old Mary did not only freeze but her whole demeanour changed. She suddenly became a gentler woman. As if young Mary herself being a neighbour with a UK passport as opposed to a Bulgarian builder meant that she deserved to be treated differently.

'Hi Mary,' said old Mary. 'I was telling Kostadin he should advise me when they are going to be using water on your terrace, because the sound of water over my head is unnerving.'

Kostadin looked at young Mary with bovine eyes as he stretched himself up, cupping his T-shirt into some sort of bowl to hold steady the debris from the gulley. He and Milen by his side smiled at her in unison, the brush and dustpan still dangling from Milen's right hand.

'We do what we can, Mary. But they have to work. They have three window frames to build and sand by the end of the week. And every so often they need to clean the dust. They can't really call you every time they put the hose on,' young Mary was attempting to make old Mary listen to reason.

Old Mary groaned almost an imperceptible groan, and Kostadin and Milen shifted slightly. 'But Kostadin had promised he would call me directly and he didn't,' she said.

Young Mary was surprised Kostadin had old Mary's phone number, and a touch jealous. He hadn't mentioned getting her neighbour's details. She looked at old Mary's face and thought again how she looked ancient, way past sixty. *Must be the life of the camps,* she thought. *No risk a lover could ever wake up next to her to be surprised he had fucked a minor.* And the colour shade of her hair, platinum blonde, looked ridiculous. Next, Kostadin seemed to be about to say something but was interrupted.

'Look at this,' old Mary told young Mary pointing to the floor. 'I come here three days a year and my whole terrace is flooded.'

All young Mary could see was a small puddle by the gulley. 'Mary,' she told old Mary, 'it was the heaviest downpour in the shortest time for three years last night. Emergency services around London are stretched. Given we never carry out any maintenance of roofs or drain pipes in this building, you are lucky to have just a puddle. I have leaks all over my apartment!'

But old Mary wasn't happy. She next pointed to a rusty metal table and chair she could not have paid more than a pound for at a salvage yard. They were trying to be red but were too rusty even for that. They were trying to cry, 'We are vintage, were born years back in a little corner of Rousillon...' but they failed at that as well. They should have simply been in the bin. Young

Mary thought she would never sit on something like that and felt certain Kostadin and Milen had better garden furniture in their houses too.

On top of the table, there was a tall glass. 'Is it too much to ask for a perfect quiet morning, with a perfect Bloody Mary?' Old Mary was pointing directly at the Bloody Mary.

Young Mary wondered if Kostadin's hand was getting infected inside all that wet debris. If his poor, marvellous fingers were tired holding the fold of his T-shirt. She would need those hands later, on her windows.

'Can your workers just work quietly?' Old Mary was pleading.

'Mary,' young Mary spoke again to old Mary. 'They have already agreed to have the radio off.'

Old Mary pouted.

'Mary,' young Mary talked to her again. 'I don't want to be doing these works any more than you do. But my windows are falling apart. The building did not want to pay for works, including yourself who voted against them. So in an emergency such as this, I got Kostadin and Milen to change my windows at my own expense in half the time scheduled under the original works, and without the harassment of erecting scaffolding,' she sighed. 'I am sorry if a bit of dust or water drops on your head but I am trying to avoid it being a whole window next time. Don't you think that's wise?' Young Mary saw Kostadin giggle out of the corner of her eye, which filled her with warmth.

'It's just I need some peace for my Bloody Mary,' retorted old Mary. 'I am nothing without one in the morning. I can't function,' she added. Suddenly she was claiming to have a Bloody Mary every day of the year – every morning in her camps?

'Sure, please, then can you lend us a plastic bag and we will take the debris from the gulley and be off?' asked young Mary.

'Why can't your builders bring their own bags?' Old Mary wouldn't budge, and the builders had become audience in a tennis match.

'Mary,' young Mary's patience was deserting her, 'Kostadin just cleaned your gulley for free. You would have had to call the building manager and wait over three weeks for building services to come out. And they would have charged us a couple hundred pounds!' The way young Mary saw it, old Mary should be kissing Kostadin's ass, not refusing him a bin bag. But Kostadin might not like that much. Neither would herself.

'Look at the flake on the windows.' Old Mary would not let it go.

Young Mary looked at the windows. Old Mary's windows were not dirty from dust or falling debris. They were rotting and needed repairing: at least a good three coats of paint.

'I have no bags to provide your builders anyway,' old Mary scowled again. 'And they come in with muddy shoes and dirty my place. I have a party tomorrow. Who will help me clean this mess? Could you please come down to help me prepare? I am all alone. I arrived back only three days ago. I am all alone. I need help.'

Young Mary saw her builders mesmerised by old Mary's pleading. She was letting herself go, quickly becoming undone. Next, young Mary looked at her builders' feet and realised for the first time they were shoeless, on the cold terrace floor. She suddenly remembered seeing their shoes by the entrance. 'It's madness,' she said. 'We're out.'

In a flash, young Mary re-started her builders into motion. Kostadin was still holding the dripping gulley's debris inside the folds of his T-shirt, and Milen put the dustpan under it, to cross old Mary's filthy living room without soiling it.

But old Mary stopped them. 'You see, because of all their mess I had to call some workers to come help me tomorrow.'

Kostadin's eyes opened large. He knew the men coming the next day. He had spoken to them at the entrance the day before. They were Bulgarian too, and they were not coming to help old Mary tidy up their mess but to cut her overgrown tree.

'And you may be able to afford paid help as a banker,' old Mary stared pleadingly at young Mary, 'but I am only a charity worker. And I am all alone.'

Just then, Kostadin noticed it first.

Something in young Mary's face shifted before she started yelling at old Mary. 'What do you know about me? About my finances? You moaning, judgemental old cow! I have no job. Zero salary. I had to leave my bank to take care of my child. And you are all alone? Try being all alone but with a child. At least I do my best, to smile, to treat people with respect, and not to live in a tip like yours.' Next she jumped at old Mary's neck.

Kostadin let the debris fall to old Mary's terrace floor and leapt to restrain young Mary, as old Mary broke into tears. 'So I'm a bad person. Now, am I a bad person?' She kept repeating again and again at Milen behind Kostadin, who was dragging young Mary out of old Mary's flat.

Back upstairs, Kostadin caressed young Mary's hand until she was calmer. He asked her to make him one of her signature espressos he loved.

Next, he and Milen went out on the terrace for a cigarette, and she saw them opening a large, strong canvas bag holding a hoover-like appliance with a long pole. It was an industrial pressure hose. 'To wash old Mary away.' Kostadin glanced back at young Mary, smiling at her wildly, and then there was a loud pneumatic hiss...

4

In the playground

The young lad arriving breathless with Annie by his hand says hello to Melissa, waiting in the school's courtyard.

She remembers two days before, when she had to bend to give Annie a hug because the toddler had gone into a frenzy, and he hadn't known what to do. *Yet another foreign male au pair,* she had judged him immediately.

It has become such a fashion amongst mums, their opening to fresh-faced, exotic strangers of the opposite sex, possibly expected to bring much-needed excitement into their lives. But Melissa would not have thought Annie's mum to be that kind.

The lad moves across the yard to rest his lean butt on the school's rear wall and lets Annie loose as they wait for her brother – in Melissa's son's same class – to come out. Annie meanders past Melissa, directionless.

'How are you, Annie?' Melissa gently caresses the toddler's cheek and the girl grimaces back at her. *She has always had a temper,* thinks Melissa. *The poor au pair must have his hands full with her.* She sees he's looking straight at them.

'Thank you for the other day,' he says to Melissa, who walks to him to extend him a handshake.

'I'm Jack's mother, Melissa. My son is in class with Annie's brother Leo.'

'I'm Michael,' he replies with the hint of a foreign accent. But Melissa is not good with accents. 'I am Annie's father's nephew and will take care of Annie and Leo for a couple of months, until the summer.'

Melissa nods.

'Or try to,' he adds.

They both laugh.

Soon Jack is running out of the school's door like a bull they've let into the ring. He immediately dumps his coat and bags onto Melissa. 'Can we go to the park, Mum?' He seems desperate.

'Sure,' she says.

Leo is besides Jack in a flash. Annie runs to give her brother a big hug.

'Cute,' whispers Melissa.

'Michael, Michael, can we go to the park with them?' asks Leo.

Michael turns to Melissa. 'Do you mind?'

'Of course not.'

Melissa usually takes Jack to the park in front of their apartment but, she has to admit, it's not a great park. In fact, Jack often gets bored within twenty minutes there. But that suits her, given their overcrowded schedule. As things stand, they often end up having to cram homework, bath and dinner all in one hour; she wonders how other mums do it. But she suddenly feels embarrassed to drag Michael, Annie and Leo all the way to that park nearer her house than theirs, which has so little to offer. 'Which park do you normally take them too?' she asks Michael.

'There's one not far from our house,' he replies, pensively.

'Yes, yes the one with the games!' Leo is shouting.

Melissa agrees that sounds super and they set off in the opposite direction to her home. But after twenty minutes of dragging foul-humoured Annie through rows and rows of identical, tree-lined, suburban-looking terraced houses, and shouting (quietly) at the boys, speeding like hunting beasts ahead, not to scream too loud themselves and to stop at every crossing, they still have not reached the park. It's a gruelling hot day for early May.

When they finally arrive to their destination, it's new for Melissa. She admits she had been this side of the school before with other mums but they had always gone to a different park. 'Never to this one,' she tells Michael.

There is nothing wrong with this park.

In fact, once she gets her bearings, Melissa believes it is even connected to the one she has gone to before. Except that the kids' play area in this park appears to be inside what looks like a huge fenced cage. Melissa has a sudden primordial fear, as if this cage were the kind of hotel there's no checking out of once you have checked in. Michael pushes the door to the cage, and two fat, black girls sitting by a worn-out blue plastic table stare at him.

'Kids' names?' the oldest, barely fifteen perhaps, asks Michael, sounding almost automated.

'Leo,' he replies, then looks at Melissa.

She's still trying to understand how this works, assessing whether the teenagers at the table are officially in charge or have only self-nominated in a dishonest attempt to make a bit of money from naive parents. She realises Michael hasn't been here before either, which makes her even more uneasy. 'How does this work?' Melissa enquires, fixating the youngest of the two register girls as she is writing down Leo's name on her scrunched piece of paper.

The older girl sends Melissa and Michael an offended glance and points to an official-looking certificate taped to the front of their plastic table. Melissa notices her nails are expensive acrylic with fake diamond studs; unbelievable! *Thank God I have a boy,* she acknowledges to herself.

The alleged legal document she has been directed to has the council's logo and a set of rules on it. The activities in the enclosure, beyond the reception point Melissa and Michael are standing at, are for kids from four to twelve years old only, and can be used for free. Kids are to be registered at the entrance of the playground. Adults are not allowed in. They can either state a time when they will come back to collect their kids, or wait on the other side of the fence. And they are required to leave a phone number.

Melissa is embarrassed to have caused offence and sees Jack and Leo are getting impatient, eager to disappear inside the enclosure. She can't see where the park extends to though; she can't see who or what games are inside. 'Jack is his name,' she says, pointing out her son to the register girl holding the pen. Then she turns to Michael. 'I guess Annie can't go in, she's too little.'

'How old is she?' The younger girl is asking.

'Four,' Michael lies.

'Then she can.'

'Take care of her,' Michael says as he hands Annie to Leo, who pulls her inside behind him, following Jack.

The kids soon disappear from the adults' view and Melissa can barely recognise the shades of their little bodies in the distance. She tries not to agonise too much, but she's thinking back to a story she read recently where a father was accidentally locked inside a deserted playground with his two young girls, unable to ask for help, and they ended up having to kill and eat a pigeon.

'Let's take to that bench.' Michael points to a bench opposite the cage's entrance, facing the fence, and Melissa follows him.

'Have you always lived in London?' Melissa asks Michael once they are seated, to make conversation. He explains he's taking time off from his studies in the US.

'What are you studying?'

'Law. I should graduate next year,' he says.

'You have any plans afterwards?'

'I would like to specialise in children's law.'

Melissa nods, almost without registering Michael's answer.

'Taking care of Annie and Leo is only temporary,' he adds, 'because my uncle asked me to give his wife a hand.'

His wife would be Annie and Leo's mum, Begita, thinks Melissa. 'Cool,' she says.

Then there is silence and Michael pretends to be reading a piece of paper he has taken out from his pocket.

Melissa looks around.

She could take out her book and read. It may not be construed as rude. She has seen that done before by many mums, not to other mums but to nannies. Plenty of times. Is an *au pair* a nanny even if he almost has a university degree? Even if he is a relative of Leo's and Annie's dad? There is a twenty-year gap between her and Michael and they have no common interests to talk about. And even if she's trying to be nice to him, like a Good Samaritan, she can't help thinking that he's weird. Why has he appeared in London so suddenly? Do US universities give time off for this kind of experience mid-term? It seems a waste to her. Either that or there is something he's not telling her. Is Michael really studying law? Is he running away from something, recovering following some tragic event? Begita has always been such a relaxed, kind soul, the type to collect misfits and invite them in, especially if her husband asks her to; she's so committed to him. Melissa is almost certain Michael has nothing to do with Begita's own relief or amusement. Is she just being paranoid? She knows she always has strange feelings about people and then they turn out to be right and scare her!

Suddenly, a nanny speaking some Germanic-sounding language on her phone comes to sit at the end of the bench next to Melissa. The nanny takes a toddler out of the pram she has come pushing – *The same age as Annie, give or take,* thinks Melissa – then lets the little girl run free. At least she's taking care of her, despite being on the phone, Melissa tells herself, and has not put the girl in the play-cage like they have done to Annie. Annie could by now have fallen out of a tree, or eaten a couple of slugs she picked from the soil where a fox peed last night, for all they know. Or perhaps their kids are being bullied by older kids as they sit relaxing on the bench. Melissa had seen some older kids in there when they dropped theirs off, big, rough kids, she seems to remember. Perhaps the cage is established as a breeding ground for ignorant, fat, ugly urban trash of all shades, dialects and hats; future redheads, benefit-fraud slickers, and unskilled rats. She wishes she could stop fretting so elaborately and decides to try to talk to Michael again. 'How come you decided to take your time off in London – do you have friends here?' she asks.

'Not really,' he shrugs. 'I know nobody here. Except a nice Australian girl I met the other week at the skateboard ramps. We may grab dinner tomorrow,' Michael's tone is hopeful. 'And you,' he adds looking at Melissa.

She shivers at Michael calling her his friend. 'Let me have a look at where the kids are.' She stands up and walks to the fence, pressing her face against it and hurting her eyes in an effort to see beyond the possible. After about ten minutes, she sees Jack passing through like a shot arrow. She feels calmer and goes back to the bench.

Melissa forces herself to reinitiate conversation with Michael. 'Children's law...' She lets the words linger.

She had hoped Michael would have hit it off with the German nanny during her brief absence from the bench, but she's still on the phone. And her toddler seems to be pleading with her to take off her coat. The kid must be so hot in that coat. But the nanny is too busy mouthing down her mobile and Melissa feels sorry for the little baby who looks about to pass out, sweating all around her neck and narrowing her eyes to protect them from the blaring sun. Should she say something? Ask Michael to swap places so they let the nanny come over to the more shaded part of the bench?

She then realises Michael is looking at her expectantly. 'Children's law,' she repeats, 'is that mainly custody cases?' Melissa does not know much about law. Her husband owns a gambling company. She knows he has many lawyers working for him but nothing other than that.

'I would like to learn the legal-psychological approach to work with traumatised abused children.' Michael's voice sounds deep and steady and Melissa senses her own throat muscles harden. 'It's everywhere,' he adds.

He must mean the trauma. 'Sadly,' says Melissa.

She's suddenly yearning for reassurance, that Michael is a humane, normal, centred adolescent without a history of child-killing. Just another inconsiderate twat talking child abuse when they have just let their children loose in a place which, for all she knows, could well be a magnet for paedophiles, kiddie murderers and who knows what. Then she roars inside at her own thoughts. Her latest hormone regime is making her so fucking volatile!

'Look right there under that tree,' Michael whispers and points at the next bench down the line, about five metres from their own bench. 'That boy...' He looks at Melissa inquiringly. 'Six years old?'

She nods.

'Why is he playing on his own by that old man? Why is he not in the game-centre?'

Melissa is about to protest. She herself would have preferred to have Jack playing in the grass by their bench rather than in the enclosed cage which looks more prison than circus to her. 'That man looks like the grandfather to me,' she tells Michael. But on close inspection she can slowly work out that the old man looks unwashed, his hair all over the place. His boots are worn out. She could have even thought him a homeless man had she seen him on the floor by a cash machine, his hand sticking out. And the kid's school shorts are full of stains, his knees too skinny. He looks like he's quietly reading the one comic book he has ever owned.

As if the kid had noticed being noticed from afar, he unexpectedly gets up and trots towards Melissa, almost in slow motion, and hands her a stone. She smiles at him, startled, and he smiles back. The boy then looks at Michael with suspicion, but Melissa is thinking of something else, something else she has seen as the boy smiled slightly opening his mouth. It seemed to her even that small movement of his mouth pained him. And she thought she saw some blood between his two tiny front teeth. Her heart suddenly constricts. She feels very sick.

But the boy has run away.

And next to Melissa the Germanic nanny has put her phone down because the red-faced little girl by her is wailing from the heat she can't stand another minute of.

Melissa wants to go back home.

She gets up to the fence once more and shouts and shouts for Jack. She panics when nobody comes to the fence. One of the reception girls finally approaches and asks Melissa to stop shouting, then Jack appears behind her, grinning.

'We should go,' she tells him.

'No, Mum, we are having such a great time.'

'Only five more minutes,' she insists and he runs away.

Melissa is back with Michael, who has himself now taken a little book out of his satchel – had he had the bag with him all along without Melissa noticing, or has he stuck his head in some bush and suddenly come out with it?

He pretends to be reading the first chapter through pop-idol sunglasses over closed eyes. (Did the glasses come from the satchel too?) The book's cover has a child's face on it and Melissa doesn't even want to look at the title. But she can't help it.

Living Without Your Father is the title.

Next, Melissa is too intrigued, driving her to read carefully over Michael's shoulder: 'First he came with hair, then without, then never back. A child's testimony.' For Christ's sake! she thinks to herself, shivering again and Michael notices.

'You know my uncle is not Leo's father, right?' he blurts out of the blue.

Where did this come from? thinks Melissa annoyed. She doesn't want to know. She doesn't need to know. Begita is her friend and if she did not tell her, then it's none of her business. But Michael won't stop,

'He's Annie's but not Leo's dad.'

'I didn't know,' Melissa tells Michael, dead serious. It's an angry look she's wearing. *Motherfucking behold!* she is telling Michael, to cut it off. *Now!*

Michael holds Melissa's stare and she gives up before he does, because the old man by the tree is trying to get up from his bench whilst shouting at the boy. He has put his large hand around the boy's neck and is forcing him to help him up. They are going back home.

But the boy has turned to wave to Melissa, who waves back

with the boy's stone in her hand, and then all she can see is their backs as the boy strolls home with his burden, that old man he may not want to grow up with.

Melissa is almost in tears when Jack, Leo and Annie run from the door of the cage towards her bench. 'Who signed them out?' She hugs Jack against her tight, gets up and announces they have to rush home.

That night at bedtime, Jack says he has something to tell Melissa.
'Yes, darling?' She's scared.
'You know that Leo's dad is not really his dad?'
'I did not know,' she lies. 'Did he tell you today? Does it worry you?' she asks her son.
'His dad is dead. But he says it's fine. Because he loves his new dad. And they are taking him on safari until he gets over things.'
Melissa smiles and thinks to the baby girl ignored by her nanny, to the boy and the old man, to Michael and his book. She asks no more. She kisses Jack goodnight and moves upstairs, hoping to catch up on a paper she's been reading, about an inheritance tax loophole for her husband, her son can benefit from the day he dies. 'Fuck! Life's bad.'

5

Weekend escape

He's packing against the background of the white wardrobe as she stares through him, recalling how she was the one to change the knobs of its doors herself when they first bought the flat. But he doesn't look up at her, busy as he is stuffing his weekend leather bag full of pristine shirts she collected from the dry cleaner only this morning.

'So where are you off to this time?'

'Marge, don't start!' He still doesn't look at her in case she asks him for something. What would shut her up this time? Last year, after the Range Rover, she seemed ready for anything, perhaps even to terminate an unexpected pregnancy had he asked her. But he hadn't needed to, as the miscarriage came of its own accord. She must be too old for new motherhood by now.

'What an effort is a night away from home. Bleak!' She's obviously joking. 'I bet your golf is getting top-notch.' She won't let it go. 'You'll soon have enough handicap to join that damned club and leave us for good.' She smiles as if she means nothing. She always thought handicap was such a stupid word in golf, taken to measure ability when it really depicts a disability. She thinks her husband is seriously handicapped, at least when it comes to spending time with his family: he can't handle it.

He finally looks up at her. 'You are not funny.'

She can recognise in his look a desperation she has seen recently, during seldom intimate moments when he fucked her hard, possibly hoping it could bring back the way he used to desire her. She can recognise it because she has felt it herself for some time. Unexpectedly, her mobile pings inside the pocket of her yoga pants; it's a message from Pat.

He's grabbing a pair of swimming trunks.

'A golf requirement?' she teases him as Pat's message opens on her screen. She knows he thinks her aggravating when busy at knowing everything.

Charlie often takes him to funky hotels a stone's throw from the club; they always have a pool. She knows that's what his answer will be and she doesn't wait for it. She reads on her screen instead: 'Marge, Jack and I have been together for months. We just don't know how to tell you. But we want to be together. He's picking me up today at eleven.' It's a medusa sting for which Marge suddenly feels scandalously unprepared. Why?

Pat was always that kind of fish, Marge thinks after a moment. *A fish hurting other fish.* She knows nothing about medusas. *The personification of all that's put on earth only to break bonds. No one should be fooled by her glamour, and wives everywhere may by and large benefit from an anti-Pat movement taking hold.*

Then Marge tries to see the positive. At least it's not a seventeen-year-old bikini barista, not that there are many given the nation's climate. She suddenly wishes Pat had printed her confession and faxed it over though: she hates the casualness of text messages. She feels a fire starting somewhere central to her body, and her husband, Jack, has just run into the shower having proudly exclaimed, 'All packed.' He has left her alone in her yoga clothes facing her bland wardrobe wall, all white other than for the funky knobs, on a sunny Saturday morning, his weekend bag of sin resting proud like a statue on the pedestal of their unmade bed.

The whole thing feels like an installation, including me, Marge is concluding fast. *A living installation where the living part, Marge Atwood, is slowly consuming from the inside. When she's all burnt up, the installation will cease to be a piece of art. It will get dismantled and something else will take its place.*

Could Pat, who is stealing Marge's future in life, be too robbing her of an identity in death?

Marge mechanically pulls up her diary on her mobile. Twelve golf weekends so far this year. The evidence is irrefutable. Is there a yoga-based solution to sex addiction? She has already gifted her husband the taped porn Pilates collection stolen from her trainer!

What does Pat tell her own husband? She had claimed during their last social gathering at Little Social, the four of them alone, that she had taken up fishing. Marge had thought it very fishy indeed. Pat taking up fishing? A women's-only fishing club? She had never heard of fishing in the outskirts of London. What fishing? She had never been invited to try. But then she was into yoga, not fishing.

Digging into the past is not going to help anything, Marge tells herself. She feels she's still slow-burning and needs to stop it somehow, before she becomes ashes, but she can't.

Does Pat's husband, Charlie, know? Is he fine with it? He is so acceptant, does not know how to stop being honouring and honourable. Always ready to congratulate himself, Pat, Marge, Jack, in summary anybody, for what is happening in their lives, dispensing compliments as if hired by God as a keen associate to impart good. He's outright madness. What if he doesn't know?

Should Marge confront Pat? If Pat knows she knows and still leaves the door ajar, then every other woman can feel justified to come and have a try.

Should she tell Charlie? Poor sod, from the vault to the altar he took three weeks, duped by that whore. Pat's lucky he's no control freak. And what a cheek Jack is, using his lover's husband as decoy for their own filthy weekends... Marge thinks it's so unchristian. Yet so clever. Because in their social dinners, Marge talks to Pat and Jack to Charlie, and Marge has not said a word to Charlie in the past ten years. Come to think of it, she does not even have his phone number.

Marge sits by her husband's bag on the bed.

The shades of blinds, bright white and cold-looking in stripes, criss-cross her. They are like a fishnet indifferent to her turmoil; they aggravate her. She suddenly can't see into tomorrow and has to go back to the past, the best place to set up camp for now; to nests in the hay, evening smells of woodstock and saddles of Cordovan leather for her pretty horses. A safe past kindly lit where she stays until she feels loose, far away from her body.

She hears the water of the shower turn off. Jack still has to shave; she has a bit of time.

But she knows she can't think straight, her body limp on their matrimonial; it's a posture of defeat. So she springs up and lets herself fall on her hands to the floor, then into the *Eka Pada Koundinyasana* position: an existential tranquilliser. It's pretty advanced but she has been doing yoga for a few years now, on and off since the birth of Jack Junior. She fixes her gaze on her yoga stone on her right index finger, yet another of Jack's recent gifts to celebrate that they have not yet killed each other after so long. This may help her concentrate on the re-edification of her future.

Inside the bathroom, Jack Senior looks at himself nude in the mirror.

The electric light is offensive yet he feels he looks younger. His six pack is taking shape and the weights at the gym are doing wonders for his upper muscles. He only needs to work on his legs a little. Next, he paints his chin white with an expensive soap Marge gave him for Christmas. Pat gave him the same, but that tub he has just packed in his weekend bag.

All in all, he feels quite good with himself this year. He got that promotion he wanted at work and a decent bonus that made Marge and Jack Junior happy. She got the special Pilates board thingy she wanted and his son got the latest Nintendo. He thinks they are content and he has life under control at home, still managing to devote decent time to his career and his other interests. He hates couples who show an unhealthy dependence on each other...

Whilst musing, he cuts himself, distracted. It's a small cut. 'The balance is just right,' he says, inspecting his cut in the mirror. 'It hasn't been for some years but now it is.'

When he thinks about Pat, he knows it was inevitable; with her he feels a giant under the sheets. When he closes his eyes he can still see her cunt. He can go back to loving his own thoughts and watching them like a TV show. Savouring sexual acts with Pat whether in his brain or a sordid, scarcely furnished, suburban hotel, has become a main source of happiness in his life.

Marge just doesn't like sex or at least not with him, and that soon put him off himself to have sex with her. How many times has she denied him before? Not even pretending to hide her clumsiness but showing affront? Well, he too often thought her lame in bed. She failed to see rainbows for him. He tends to think they became non-coital to each other; he has totally made that term up but likes it. And the whole no-sex thing made him self-conscious, driving feelings of worthlessness, dragging him down along a vicious cycle until an eternity without sex just seemed to him too stark a destiny. Why could Marge not have made a virtue of the necessity of telling herself her husband was a good lover like any other decent woman? It would have helped.

Yes, he admits it was sexual resentment that got him to where he is now. 'Sexual fulfillment is key to healthy relationships,' Jack tells the mirror. He has fully recovered from his ordeal but perhaps he's no longer in love with Marge. He inspects his shave and reaches for the aftershave *eau de cologne*; strictly *Acqua di Parma* these days, because it makes Pat go crazy.

Jack thinks Pat is also settled now, come to understand how theirs is a win-win arrangement. She has finally parked her 'I'm my own earth where I bloom, not a hole to be ravaged for resource' complaints away, after enough cake and praise from him. Yes she's younger and gorgeous and probably he doesn't deserve her. But then, with that difficult husband of hers, who expects her to behave deferential, not to say obsequious, where else would she find an arrangement so suited to her situation?

Jack understands Charlie well. He understands what can and cannot be done and what he and Pat can get away with so that everyone is happy. Pat may have had reveries of more at some point. So has he, perhaps. But they both know it's a fantasy. And he has Marge and Jack Junior to consider; not that Jack Junior seems to care much about what he and his mum get up to these days: Jack has almost had to re-plumb his heart to bypass the hurt from the indifference his son shows him. He would still try to hold onto his marriage for the boy though; even if this may fuck his son up even more! And Marge? The thing is Marge loves him even when she teases him, he knows. And so he does love her in a way. Things work with her, outside the sex. Why break something that works? The best is to leave things as they are.

Jack starts dressing, the black Ralph polo and Armani chinos he had prepared by the towel rack.

He's thinking about the car he has hired for this weekend and how much the touch of that leather seat will turn Pat on. Of course, he has told Marge that Charlie is picking him up as usual, whilst the car awaits, parked around the corner. Yes, he feels bad about these little lies but they are just that, little lies. What difference does it make if he gets picked up or rents a luxury car for a monthly weekend escape? He can afford it anyway; he works hard; it's his money.

Finally ready, he wipes the bathroom mirror, which has steamed up again. He has a final look at himself. 'Good enough!' He feels excitement rushing up his loins.

When Jack opens his bathroom door, he sees her there, on the floor. Marge is still in the *Eka Pada Koundinyasana* position. He doesn't know the name but it looks definitely weird and unexpected given this is not her yoga room. He paid for his studio to be turned into her yoga room last year, after buying the Range Rover, for a precise reason, so that she would stop freaking him and Jack Junior out around the house. As well as to make himself feel better after starting his affair; it was kind of a redemption project.

Next Jack jockeys into Marge's axis of attention.

She loses her balance and falls to the floor. 'Bastard,' she mouths at him, 'to think you and me will one day share a headstone!' As he moves to help her up, slightly shaken by her remark, she waves him away and springs to her feet like a cheetah. Air seems to sip gradually out of her for a long moment, with very little coming back in.

Jack has to agree it's amazing what yoga or Pilates or whatever it is, perhaps just having ten hours a day to devote to your own body, has done to Marge's physical agility in the past few years.

She can certainly kick ass now. He sees her calmly move towards a chair and he sighs, resigned to see her do something even stranger on it next, like a handstand followed by a pirouette perhaps. *She could be so amazing in bed if she wanted,* he thinks. *All this good horniness wasted...* But he knows it's broken between them and he doesn't want to go over it anymore. It makes him sad to think she sees him as anything but arousing; she treats him worse than a chewing gum on the sidewalk.

When she has reached the chair, Marge grabs it with two hands and throws it violently at Jack, her grief hardly humanising her. The chair makes a loud noise against the window.

Jack is stunned, between self and soul, facing pure fucking terror. He turns to Marge, her hands on her hips, her nude feet slightly apart. She seems to be blowing air from her nostrils, preparing to charge like a bull. She's saving on expletives though, not a word coming from her mouth.

He has to stay calm. He knows if he gets agitated he will sweat and glisten.

Jack Junior comes into the bedroom without knocking, holding a gherkin. He must have been startled by the noise. He looks at his parents as if to a snapshot of loved people long dead. 'Can you keep it down, guys?'

Nobody moves. Nobody talks.

Jack Junior is suddenly forced to measure the ups and downs of the situation facing him, embracing it in any way he can.

He knows his dad is disappearing again for the weekend. He seems to have had a chair thrown at him, and the only other person in the room is his mum. His mum doesn't like his dad disappearing to play golf, he concludes.

Except Jack Junior knows his dad does not play golf. He's useless at it. Uncle Charlie told him at the last barbecue. Uncle Charlie has no children of his own and loves him. Jack Junior talks to him a lot. And he knows Uncle Charlie is not picking his dad up today, because he saw his dad park a fancy rental car round the corner yesterday as he was coming back from his friend Alex's. His dad had been fussing with the car's interior: closing the ashtray, winding the window, acting pure weirdo.

Jack Junior summarises facts in his head once again: his mum is mad at his dad because he's disappearing in a fancy car, to play something other than golf. Sounds bad. But it's okay. Jack Junior is not an idiot and he doesn't expect his parents to be pure, incorruptible and noble.

'Everything okay, guys?' he asks next.

Nobody moves. Nobody talks.

Jack Junior's dad feels a terrible collage of wounds, tumours, warts and rashes as well as his toenails flaking off, which makes him shiver. His mum yearns to hurl rocks and climb the sky.

Jack Junior knows that his mum knows that his dad doesn't play golf. Because when he last went into her computer, to disable the parental system his dad had set to have her informed of everything he watches, he found a folder named PRIVATE and naturally double-clicked to open a stream of WhatsApp screenshots between a Jack and a Pat, which he printed to keep in his trouser pocket.

He and Alex going through them could not believe how childish adults can be.

'Bloody morons!' said Jack Junior.

'Immense technological advances facilitate exchanging especially lies!' Alex reassured him. 'This age is bleak for all it allows.'

Is Jack Junior's dad an ace or an ass? Is his mum weak or a deviant? It does not matter to Jack Junior as long as they don't bother him. They never really have much.

'Anyone peckish for gherkins?' he asks ready to share his.

Still nobody moves. Nobody talks.

Jack Junior realises his mum seems REALLY mad, and his dad has the appearance of a man in prayer, a constipated man.

There must be more?

He puts his thinking hat on for one last time. He wants to solve this for his own sake; he has a lot scheduled for the weekend and welcomes no derailments of any kind. He studies the scene of the crime again...

The chair on the floor by the window. His dad, in a black polo, braces with glitter dust on top, and stupidly trendy chinos talking more lust than common decency, freshly shaven, with a small cut on the right of his chin, bleeding just a little. His brow is sweating. He definitely glistens, which makes him look weak. His mum in her enlightenment clothes in the yoga pose *Tadasana* by now, stares at his dad like she's about to kill him, unless she can think of a calming line from her fridge magnet philosophy collection. She seems made of steel. The emotional energy attracting these two bodies is so evident to Jack Junior he doesn't understand why his parents don't fuck more. He just knows they like each other but apparently things are complicated.

Beware the well-trodden path, Jack Junior thinks. *Beware the never-trodden path,* he also tells himself, as he brainstorms every option. *Suspect conclusions,* he advises. *Suspect inconclusiveness.*

Then he sees it there in front of him. His mum's phone on the floor. Somehow it has not locked itself and he can see the screen with the message from Pat. He makes a superhuman effort to read it but he doesn't even need to.

Charlie was right that day, talking against a large backdrop painting of pretty, calcareous-white churches and blood-orange renaissance palazzi he claimed had costed him a fortune at auction. He had said it all along in fact, that he was very happy with the status quo and totally trusting in Jack Junior's parents, but that he wasn't sure his wife Pat was the smart cookie she thought she was. 'She's a bit of a dud really, she could spoil things, think she can get more,' Charlie had told Jack Junior, munching some garlic bread he claimed was a substitute for his old ketamine addiction. 'But you don't need to worry because I will always be here for you,' he had added mid-caress with his garlic-bread-free hand, as Jack Junior sat calmly by a pyramid of cigarette packages on Charlie's table.

Still, Jack Junior's potential tragic life version under divorced parents suddenly comes to haunt him.

What if Charlie doesn't keep his promise?

Could he end up at an orphanage-like boarding house? No wall of Nintendo games; no clutter of Star Wars collectibles; no kitsch robotic souvenirs drawer; no hot baths; filthy carpets; living only to become a brilliant young mathematician, a prodigy. 'It's a mistake to believe that good thought simply comes when you whistle,' he imagines being told by a menacing overweight headmaster with hair out of his nostrils. He frets he would be expected to get into Oxford at fifteen; gain a doctorate at nineteen; and would have to take his life by twenty. There's danger in Jack Junior's logic but still he knows exactly what his only option is.

'Guys!' 'Guys!' he shouts until both his parents acknowledge him. 'Pay attention,' he tells them.

Next, he grabs his mum's phone, waves it around to his parents as if they both need to see it ahead of a magic trick, then presses delete, sending Pat's message to its death, as he makes each of his movements as obvious as possible. He knows there's urgent need for a serious conversation between these two people they are incapable of having, but he will make them.

'Now, you hear me, both of you,' he's staring at them. 'Let me live!'

He urges them before turning around and shutting his parents' bedroom door behind him.

6

Rico, rico

The airmail envelope weighed nothing in my hand. It had to be from my oldest aunt. Nobody used those envelopes anymore; nobody even wrote letters anymore. Her handwriting was terrible.

Her news wasn't good either, but she wasn't an alarmist. Her husband had died four years before and she was nearing seventy-five and alone. We hadn't travelled to my uncle's funeral because it was far to travel to Cartagena. And because we had lost touch with my aunt after my grandmother died; my father, my aunt's brother, had faded from her life and so had I, her godson. In reality, we hadn't been very close before Granny's death either, given Aunty had forever, since I can remember, lived in Colombia. Grandmother had been the anchor bringing us all together once a year, and still we had missed many such reunions. I myself recalled travelling to her all the way to Cartagena only once before.

My aunt's letter said she intended to leave her wealth to me after her death but she could not be bothered to make a will; she didn't trust lawyers. She did not believe in inheritance law and the government would steal everything through tax anyway, she claimed. Her letter insisted she wanted my name on her bank account. I would then empty it the minute she left this world. *How bad would that look!* I laughed out loud as I read her letter.

She also mentioned she had some family jewels for me. It was odd given I am a boy, and as far as I knew she had no idea of my sexual orientation. Would she turn out old-fashioned enough to care? She should not. I was convinced that with time, there would be no more distinct boys and girls in this world, that we would all become sex-neutral assholes if civilisation continued its crazy course. But was she of the same opinion?

In summary, my aunt seemed readying herself for a goodbye but did not come through at all pressured in her letter. Did she not at least want to see what I had become before she carked it, before she left me everything? She must have. If you studied between the lines, she proposed for me to travel all the way to her for my name to be put on her account, as if it could not be achieved any other way.

I read the letter alone in my living room.

I was an associate in a big corporate law firm in London at the time and so was my partner, though we hardly saw each other. I called him a sucker for toiling like he did when he could earn the same working less, like I somehow managed to.

He was invariably exhausted. I was often alone.

I had asked him to take a break with me that May, far away, and he had said it was not a good time; he would be on an unmissable training that particular week followed by a team-building weekend at a big partner's villa in Provence. I had demanded he cancelled it, ordered him to reschedule. He had said no to both, making me question whether there was more than ambition to it, whether he feared we looked ridiculous together, would never want to hold my hand in public. Perhaps he was only intending to stand his ground and pretend he could never be forced into commitments.

Looking at Aunt's letter, I told myself I should open to adventure. I must have felt deep in my heart that I should see her. I didn't care about the jewels. I didn't wear any. I wouldn't sell any. Or the money. It may be hard to believe but I was naive enough back then to suppose that I would continue to increase my earning power exponentially. I had done well; I was in no need of money. It was all more simple and immediate than future profit. Perhaps all I wanted was a holiday; only the prospect of a faraway vacation keeping me alive all of a sudden. And I didn't want to feel guilty once my aunt died, that I hadn't gone to see her when she had asked me specifically.

I called my father to tell him.

Would he like to join me on the trip?

His health was shaky, he implied pointedly as if it was partly my fault. He had not talked to Aunt for years, and last time he had called her, when her husband died, he could not understand what she was saying, he claimed.

Dad sounded scared.

I understood, I told him.

Still, I had made my mind up. I had booked the flights and a nice boutique hotel for my stay, excited as if I were embarking on a heart conquest, almost readying to seduce Aunty. Because this was the other thing, I would show my aunt the new me. And she would have to be proud. We were going to recover lost time and enjoy ourselves, more than my partner would in his weekend in Provence.

In Cartagena, the boutique hotel turned out to be a collection of pastel yellow blocks in the pedestrian centre, facing the cathedral. It was postcard-pretty although I would have liked more flowers.

The place was full of fat, tipping Americans who hardly fit in the tiny, ever-glowing lift, but would never, God forbid, walk up the stairs, even to the first floor. The lift operated using a security card slot. The bellman insisted from my arrival to never let anyone in with me, as if my life depended on it. 'Everyone has a gun here.' He told me the welcoming news with a wide smile, showing a gold tooth. He would ask for a handsome tip for that piece of information later.

My room was heavy on oak furniture and matching yellow paint and fabrics. I opened the lemon curtains to find a pretty view of the street below, across thick iron safety bars. At least I could hear the bells of the cathedral. I could not see the church from my room but I could hear the bells in its tower.

On further exploration, I found a Jacuzzi corner on the third floor with partial visibility of the church and two potted geraniums, which made me feel happier. I also met another couple of elderly Americans claiming to be on a cruise stop, who assured me the breakfast was phenomenal. This place will be fine for three days, I thought.

After a nap I messaged my aunt to let her know I had arrived safely. She had unwillingly left a tide of incomprehensive voicemails on my room's answering machine, where she thought she was talking to me, and seemed increasingly angry I didn't respond to her questions. Her recorded voice sounded zombie-like and I suffered from a momentary lack of confidence... Still, the whole point of having come here was to visit her. Was it not? Thus I started to program my visit to her flat, like a military operation.

When I had last come to stay with my uncle and aunt in their condo at the age of eight, if I remembered correctly, they had been the first to advise us of the dangers of the city and the violence around where they lived. So I decided that I would not rely on public transport this time, but it would be strictly taxis for three days. It was only three days and it was not as if I could not afford it. I would also report my every move back to my partner in Europe, with clear instructions in case he didn't hear from me. I was perhaps paranoid. And I knew my partner would be a reluctant collaborator at best, given he was the relaxed type even when he wasn't with workmates in Provence. But having him involved, if only theoretically, somehow made me feel safer.

At my aunt's condo, the main gate was shut with two sets of pointed iron bars. She asked me, through the buzzer, to make sure nobody was following me in. I buzzed again at the entrance of her building and at her apartment door, coming through a new set of bars each time. It was the stuff of movies, and it was making me nervous when I most needed to ease into our long-awaited reunion.

Aunt looked a frail relic, way worse than anything I had expected. It didn't help that she had greeted me in her nightie, a bathrobe on top. It was my granny's old nightie too, making me hold back a sudden urge to cry. But she pushed me inside hurriedly, then took about ten minutes to lock the bar behind me and then her door. Anyone who wanted to, could have easily killed us before we were safe inside.

I hugged her.

She cut the hug short and directed me to her sofa; I could swear a déjà vu. Either that or it was the same sofa she had had when I had visited age eight. In fact, as I looked around, nothing seemed much different to how I remembered it from all those years ago, although by staying the same, everything seemed to have become old and out of place. Or perhaps my mind was playing tricks, recovering from the initial shock. Still, I was relieved I was lodging at the hotel.

'You could have stayed here,' my aunt muttered as she sat on an armchair by a small table inches from her television set which was on at top volume. 'I would have provided some sheets even if I'm not up to cooking anymore, so it's each on their own here,' she added.

I didn't remember my aunt ever cooking. Her speech was slow and sounded much more rusty than on the phone to me when I had called from London to announce my visit. She had trouble talking and her mouth dribbled a lot. She must have been making an extraordinary effort during her voicemail messages and that was making me nervous when I most needed to ease into our long-awaited reunion.

Aunt looked a frail relic, way worse than anything I had expected. It didn't help that she had greeted me in her nightie, a bathrobe on top. It was my granny's old nightie too, making me hold back a sudden urge to cry. But she pushed me inside hurriedly, then took about ten minutes to lock the bar behind me and then her door. Anyone who wanted to, could have easily killed us before we were safe inside.

I hugged her.

She cut the hug short and directed me to her sofa; I could swear a déjà vu. Either that or it was the same sofa she had had when I had visited age eight. In fact, as I looked around, nothing seemed much different to how I remembered it from all those years ago, although by staying the same, everything seemed to have become old and out of place. Or perhaps my mind was playing tricks, recovering from the initial shock. Still, I was relieved I was lodging at the hotel.

'You could have stayed here,' my aunt muttered as she sat on an armchair by a small table inches from her television set which was on at top volume. 'I would have provided some sheets even if I'm not up to cooking anymore, so it's each on their own here,' she added.

I didn't remember my aunt ever cooking. Her speech was slow and sounded much more rusty than on the phone to me when I had called from London to announce my visit. She had trouble talking and her mouth dribbled a lot. She must have been making an extraordinary effort during her voicemail messages and that

After a nap I messaged my aunt to let her know I had arrived safely. She had unwillingly left a tide of incomprehensive voicemails on my room's answering machine, where she thought she was talking to me, and seemed increasingly angry I didn't respond to her questions. Her recorded voice sounded zombie-like and I suffered from a momentary lack of confidence... Still, the whole point of having come here was to visit her. Was it not? Thus I started to program my visit to her flat, like a military operation.

When I had last come to stay with my uncle and aunt in their condo at the age of eight, if I remembered correctly, they had been the first to advise us of the dangers of the city and the violence around where they lived. So I decided that I would not rely on public transport this time, but it would be strictly taxis for three days. It was only three days and it was not as if I could not afford it. I would also report my every move back to my partner in Europe, with clear instructions in case he didn't hear from me. I was perhaps paranoid. And I knew my partner would be a reluctant collaborator at best, given he was the relaxed type even when he wasn't with workmates in Provence. But having him involved, if only theoretically, somehow made me feel safer.

At my aunt's condo, the main gate was shut with two sets of pointed iron bars. She asked me, through the buzzer, to make sure nobody was following me in. I buzzed again at the entrance of her building and at her apartment door, coming through a new set of bars each time. It was the stuff of movies, and it call last month.

'Feel free to visit around the city as you want but I hardly leave home anymore,' or something to that effect she added in words that sounded deformed almost beyond understanding, and glanced back to her screen after that. She didn't seem either pleased or offended I wasn't staying with her.

'So how have you been?' I asked over the television conversation, having given myself a moment to blend in.

It was a Latino day-show for housewives she was devouring, where they take their partner to some kind of fake court of second-class actors and cameramen, and a female judge makes them repent, hug each other in a rain of forged tears and seek advice. My aunt, once a feminist and psychiatrist for battered wives, seemed to be loving it. It saddened me. My aunt's sisters and her cousins had always held her in great esteem, as the intellectual one of the family who had escaped to specialise in America after her medicine degree. Such feats were unheard of for a woman in Spain at the time of my aunty. She had concentrated on her career and gained two degrees but birthed no kids and that was fine. But what had it all come too... 'I have been good, you see,' her delayed response came in a mumble, eyes on her television set.

'Good' was not what I saw and I felt somehow tricked. In panic, I got up from the sofa to walk to the terrace, passing behind her. I walked slowly, repeating to myself that everything was indeed good, fine. But I was trembling. I hadn't expected what I had found. I needed some air.

The terrace's floor cement was painted green. Me and my sister had played games on my aunt's terrace as kids and my mind started running tricks again. I had a view of the pool; we had one day during our holiday found a large iguana which had fallen in whilst we were swimming. Such a scare but so many laughs too. It was all different now though, and I could not escape this different reality. I had no choice but to go back inside, where I saw my aunt making an obvious effort to stand from her chair. She asked if I was hungry.

'Not really.' I did not want her to fuss over me. 'But can I help you?' I glanced to her kitchen, opening at the back of the living room. It was a mess. I wasn't even sure if I would be able to operate in there, perhaps after we scrubbed for a couple of days... I suddenly wished my mother was with me; she would know what to do. I had thought I had grown into a strong reliable man who could take care of anything, but I could not sort out what I saw in front of me and I felt frozen.

What had I expected?

That my aunt had called me to take me out in the Cartagena night scene?

I had been stupid. A selfish, naive idiot. People who don't call you for a lifetime only call you when they need you. I was looking down as I thought my thoughts, to my aunt's feet being dragged slowly by her frail legs towards a kitchen cupboard. Her slippers were hideous.

'Who makes you what to eat?' I asked her.

She explained she had someone who brought her groceries once every three days, then fetched a tin of almonds from the cupboard. It was one of those tins that opens easily but she struggled to open it nevertheless, then offered me some nuts as we walked back into the living room. 'Rico, rico,' she said sounding like a slowed down parrot as she ran the almonds between her spiderweb fingers into her mouth.

'Is this what you eat mostly?'

She shrugged, unhappy. As if implying, sometimes. As if implying that she was old enough to eat what she wanted. Then she sat back down by the television set and took off her bathrobe to reveal sagging arms over the sleeveless nightie. It was hot. 'I go out once a week, to the hairdresser,' she explained determined, even if I hadn't asked her.

I counted thirteen separate stains on her nightie, all a similar yellow colour. Perhaps it was pineapple juice. She used to buy me and my sister a lot of pineapple juice when we had been to visit all those years ago. I was glad if she was at least having vitamins.

'Cati takes me,' she added about her hairdresser trips. Cati turned out to be a man's name, my dead uncle's nephew. 'And I have all the phone numbers I may need in there,' she pointed at a small table at the side of the sofa where I had taken my seat again. Perhaps she wanted to assure me she had her care covered, or prove the opposite. There was a telephone with a large-sized keyboard, and a paper list of numbers besides it, in my aunt's handwriting; I could not understand one of them.

'It may be a good idea to organise some extra help, a cleaner perhaps?' I sounded embarrassed proposing. Because I had been there for a little more than five minutes; because the last time I had seen my aunt *she*, a responsible adult, had been telling *me*, a clueless kid, what to do. It would be obvious to any logical mind that everything had dramatically changed, but I still was finding it hard to operate the other way round. *Emotions mangle logic,* I told myself.

'This is a good bit,' she suddenly visibly cheered up indicating something on screen, and it seemed as if I was getting the hang of her slurred voice.

'Or a cook perhaps, for some hot meals?' I insisted following on from my previous suggestion but still treading lightly. Even if she lived in a hot country I believed hot meals were a must.

'I have some ready meals I like and I have trouble eating most things anyway,' she shot a swift (as fast as she could manage) reply, looking my way, then went back to the screen.

Maybe I was relieved of my aunt refusing help.

Because there was so much to do and I had come for three days only. And I had no intention of staying to sort her life out. Did I owe her that? I certainly believed that I did not. Did she think I did? She certainly was not demanding it straight. She did not seem to care.

'But I want to go to the bank tomorrow,' she added sternly, her voice clean this once, her eyes back on mine. 'I have arranged to go to the bank tomorrow. Cati will come to take us, at eleven.' Her words seemed clear and final.

After a few minutes my aunt got up again and it was distressing to watch how much pain it took for her to move even in small steps, to walk to places and fetch things. She took some papers from a shelf on the wall and moved back to her table by the television.

She asked me to pull up a chair next to her.

'They will put your name on my account,' she said shuffling her papers in front of me, 'and when something happens you just take it all out. It's the simplest way,' she insisted. 'Simpler than a will.'

Of course, I could never do such a thing, even if I couldn't deny feeling flattered she had chosen me. I remained silent for a second. 'What about finding someone locally that could manage your expenses?' I talked as if the words were burning me. I hated suggesting to her how to organise her own affairs when she had once been so able and so proud. 'Because if something happens to you,' I hesitated again, 'someone will need to take care and I will be miles away. I may not be able to come all the way here,' I waited for a reaction. 'Perhaps Cati should have his name on your account?' I attempted reasoning with her without pushing too much.

My aunt made a sound like a donkey's bray at my proposal. 'You know he says he's in love with me?' she told me.

I thought I had not understood her words at first. She was talking presumably about Cati, who was forty years her junior. She seemed serious. I gave her a sceptical look and felt wretchedness inside again, eating my gut.

'Every week he gets angry when the hairdresser compliments me.' She was all garble again, not making any sense. 'Because the hairdresser would like me to marry him, because I am a proper madam,' she added fully convinced, 'unlike all the fat ugly old *indias* of this city.' Since when had my aunt become racist? 'And Cati gets so jealous. He claims he's in love with me too but I know I can't trust him. He wants my money. He's just another young Colombian thug.'

I burst out with nervous laughter.

When my aunt decided to get up again, I told her to please remain seated.

'What are you looking for?' I asked.

She directed me to a hole under the kitchen sink. The cupboard was filthy and smelled damp. She said there was a little bundle inside an old jumper. It felt wet and alive, as if it were filled with maggots. I brought it to her. Then she turned the television off and opened the jumper over the table, as if she were unveiling a treasure: it was the family jewels. They were in a bad state. The gold looking black, the gems faded. 'Have a look at them?' my aunt urged me as she kept munching her almonds. '*Rico, rico.*'

My heart sat heavy on my knees. I had seen my grandmother wearing some of those jewels I was holding in my hands, but they had looked nothing like it.

'They are for you, I want you to have them,' my aunt told me in slow motion. That flattery again.

'Are you sure? What about giving them to your female nieces?'

'For you. Yes, yes absolutely. They are mine and they were always for you.' She winked at me.

'I will have them repaired and cleaned back in London. It's an honour to have them,' I tried my best to hide my sorrow, wrapping the jewels back inside their bundle as if they were a dead pet I had once loved.

'He was such an idiot,' she suddenly spit venom, about her husband presumably. Some of those jewels had been bought by my uncle.

I was taken aback. I searched for a trace of empathy somewhere in her words but they were factual and pointed like a dart, with nothing more behind them.

'He kept moving faster and faster up those stairs,' she pointed at her front door, presumably referring to the building stairs outside. 'Always faster records,' she seemed only slightly agitated, 'and one day, pop. He died. He fell on the floor. A neighbour found him.' She drew a line across the table with her arthritic hand. That was all she was going to say on the subject.

I only nodded.

'What time do you have to go?' she asked me next. 'You should be back early tomorrow for the bank.'

She wasn't going to let me forget that. And I felt extremely thankful that she was giving me a way out. Perhaps she wanted me out too, because our meeting had been emotionally tiring for her also. She directed me to her list of numbers to phone a cab.

None worked.

I tried the card I had been given in the hotel, by the bellman I had tipped ten dollars. But nobody answered either. I left a message.

Next, we sat for about ten minutes, with nothing to talk about. My aunt put the television set back on.

As time passed I considered walking to the bus stop, supposedly five minutes away, to get back to my hotel. But my aunt didn't recommend it. I was sure it was fine, that she lived stuck in the past and things weren't that bad anymore, street-violence-wise. But what if something happened? I suddenly felt I didn't want to die in a foreign country. Even if I had been toying with the idea of leaving my partner, I unexpectedly yearned for the chance of a full life with him. Out of the blue, I had so much to give, to become. I didn't want to die in the streets of Cartagena, alone.

'Everyone has a gun here,' my aunt said me coldly.

Then she offered to walk me out to her next-door neighbour to ask him for a ride into town, and I was mortified.

I had wanted to show to my aunt I had grown into a reliable, self-assured man. Yet I could not take care of her, not even of myself in this country. It is then that walking out of the flat, I saw a little oil portrait, by the door, on the wall. It was my grandmother. It made me feel serene for an instant despite my inner chaos, a life raft. It was definitely the only thing of value I would have ever wanted from my aunt.

At the neighbour's, a plump dark housewife with fancy big glasses, large pearl earrings and red lips under her moustache, opened her door a little and talked to us through her gate. It was identical to my aunt's gate but painted a light green rather than the standard white in most other apartments.

My aunt, still in her nightie, demanded that the woman let us through and call her husband. I noticed her voice was steadier than it had been with me, although she still dribbled from the effort of conversing. And the woman treated my aunt back as she would probably treat her own mother, mocking her slightly but surely showing her respect too, whilst I was blushing as I tried to explain the taxi situation, that taxis somehow seemed to refuse to come to this condo beyond the end of the world.

'Of course, taxis never wanna come here,' the woman explained sounding almost accusatory, in a thick accent.

Next she asked me and my aunt to please come into her apartment and wait on her sofa in the living room, under a huge oil painting attempting to take us back to the days of the *conquistadores*; perhaps Colón's boats. It was terrible. All other objects I could see around similarly tried to speak of some kind of opulence but simply talked of bad taste. Even the walls were coloured lilac under a partial wallpaper pattern trending to regal.

The neighbour abandoned us with the excuse to call her husband from his nap.

'These people are nice and helpful but pretty thick,' my aunt said clearly as she sat by my side, not even trying to whisper.

Shortly after, the housewife came back from the depths of her apartment with a pregnant teenager.

'She's my daughter,' she explained. 'My Javier can't drive you,' she talked next, directly to me. 'He says he's not going to town today for his music.'

Just then Javier appeared behind his wife, defiant. He was by far the most good-looking in the family although it was not difficult. He instructed his wife to sit by my aunt and he sat by my side, all in a line on the sofa, whilst the daughter took a nearby chair. I caressed the sofa's material and knew instantly it could efficiently light a fire that may spread speedily enough to burn the whole condo in record time, down to the washing machines in the basement. (I had thought it hilariously peculiar the time I had visited years back, how my uncle had taken me to the basement for the laundry, but I could bet the arrangement hadn't changed.)

Javier suddenly started talking as if it were only me and him in the room, man to man.

He said that my aunt was really sick, that they had been helping but she now needed family near her and they were so happy that I had come to Cartagena.

'But after so many years not seeing your aunt, you come to a hotel?' Javier's wife stepped into the conversation uninvited, her head popping out from behind my aunt's body, but Javier signalled her to shut up.

I was aghast.

I had never seen these people before in my life.

They knew nothing about me, only that they had expected me to come all the way from London, clearly to take care of my aunt.

My aunt had suddenly gone deaf and presumably heard nothing.

The couple's daughter sat in front of us reading a magazine.

Javier's wife talked again, pointing to her daughter. 'She's having a baby so we will have no time for your aunt.' Javier signalled to her again to shut up.

I was being cornered.

I offered a poker smile and got up. 'Don't worry about the taxi,' I said to my aunt.

Suddenly, a truly good-looking, albeit in a devilish way, young man, appeared out of nowhere down the corridor, like a prince materialising when you need but least expect him. 'I'm driving downtown,' the man said to the couple's daughter.

'Roberto!' my aunt called him by name before he had even acknowledged us. 'You take my nephew,' she said to him.

Roberto looked me up and down. 'With pleasure,' he replied.

I had no clue who Roberto was. If I had to guess, he seemed the kind of gorgeous asshole ready to rob you of everything, then invite you to your own stuff's launch party like you couldn't be luckier. And you would still kiss him anywhere he wanted. I wasn't going to argue with him or Aunty, and I left my aunt's neighbour's apartment with Roberto, after throwing him a lame look that said, 'I'll go back with you but I'm not promising anything' but failed to make it believable in the least.

Roberto's car was a huge 4x4. Very shiny. Black and with an ostentatious interior. Once inside, Roberto explained he was my aunt's neighbour's daughter's boyfriend, but not the father of her child. Then he asked me where my hotel was.

'*El Convento* by the cathedral in the old centre.'

He was impressed, more than my aunt had been. He asked me what I did for a living.

'Corporate lawyer.'

'Where?'

'London.'

He put some passionate music on, the type I had snogged to at age fourteen, back where I grew up in Spain.

I smiled at him.

He picked a lane and stayed in it.

He asked me what I carried wrapped in my aunt's jumper and I did not answer. Gradually, the music filled the car; it was intoxicating in my emotional state. 'Would you like to go out for dinner?' Roberto seemed unexpectedly kind.

I did not want to be rude to him until he had deposited me safe in my hotel. Did Roberto carry a gun in his glove compartment? *Everyone has a gun here*, I thought to myself after my aunt's words. I was thankful for Roberto's ride. But I was also frightened. I hadn't wanted to die on the pavements around my aunt's condo, nor did I want to in this car on a potholed road. *What the fuck*, I thought, then answered, 'Sure.' In any case, I didn't want to be alone after the day I had had.

We went somewhere not far from my hotel, me and Roberto. I could have legged it if I wanted to at that point but I did not.

Roberto bought two rum and cokes at the bar's counter. Then two more and two more after that. He seemed to know the barman. We stood outside. Kamikaze insects bombarded the little street lamps. We exchanged jokes but talked of nothing. Then we went up the stairs of the adjacent art gallery which sold nice paintings, 'Frivolous art for ten times the price a poor bastard earned making it,' Roberto clarified. He said it was his friend's gallery and that he had a room upstairs.

In the room, Roberto took the next logical step to make me his; he tried to fuck me. But he could not get it up, perhaps tired from alcohol intoxication. Next, he put on the flat screen in front of the bed, set it to a cockfight channel; claiming it often helped but it didn't then.

So we stayed hugging and caressing for about an hour, nude on the bed, then he walked me to my hotel. I didn't invite him inside the glowing lift because the bellman was watching him like a hawk.

Upstairs, in my room, I calculated it would be a good time to call Provence. I phoned my partner and cried. Then told him all was fine and hung up.

Next morning at ten thirty, Cati, my aunt's nephew, was waiting at reception. The bellman was still there, as if he had never slept. He was watching Cati like a hawk too. Cati was wearing the ocean-blue jumper he had described in his message and we walked out together. He said he had parked his car two streets down. 'An azure old *Buick LeSabre*,' he announced with pride.

The car was past its lifetime, a monster falling apart. 'Not as good as your hotel?' he asked acknowledging my surprise, a toothpick between his rotting teeth. He had the look of a small-time rascal, one that had not eaten in weeks, far from Roberto's sophisticated take on corruption. Cati could have been either a drug addict or diseased or both. And I felt we could have been in *West Side Story*.

'Get in,' he said. 'We need to pass by my home,' he explained once in the car.

I was scared, again, and the delicious hotel pancakes were rushing up and down my pipe making me feel nauseous. The American cruising couple had been right about the breakfast, but I was still fragile from the shocks of the day before: the visit to my aunt had blown my mind away, and my stomach.

I drove away with Cati, from nice picturesque streets through borderline run-down roads to derelict alleys no one in their right mind would choose to live in.

My stomach tightened further into something the size of a golf ball. My esophagus dried. Then Cati parked his rickety monster underneath a structure resembling a run-down prison and told me to stay inside the car. He got out, locking all the doors.

'Put up your window,' he shouted once outside, as he walked towards the building. He winked.

In two minutes of pure anxiety, I counted five bad-looking apes passing too close to the car in different directions. But then, all men I had met on this trip so far appeared menacing. I suddenly remembered my mobile did not work for calls abroad; I had not advised the phone company. And there was nobody I could call to help me in Cartagena. I tried to remember the national emergency number, from my aunt's list, but my memory came back blank and all I saw was her terrible handwriting. I was sweating when I opened the car's glove compartment, hoping to find what? Some reassurance? And there it was. A gun.

I closed the compartment quickly. 'Everyone has a gun here,' I said. 'Everyone has a gun.' I wanted to cry, but remembered it doesn't get you anywhere.

Then I saw Cati coming out from the building and approaching the car. I forced myself to forget about the gun.

We stopped to pick up my aunty.

She was elegantly dressed and looked almost like a living person, making me think, only if she had a reason to live, if someone took care of her everyday, she may have had another twenty years in her. *But I can't. I won't.* I couldn't. Even if it seemed a suitable arrangement for all the people concerned and

I could tell they all kind of expected it. Why? 'Cause she's your godmother!' they would say. Is it not supposed to be the other way round? Your godmother takes care of you!

I was thirty and the last time I had properly seen my aunt I had been eight. *I have a life ahead of me. Marriage (perhaps?), children (really?). A career.* I glanced at my aunt in the rearview mirror.

Did she really think she could put money on the table and I would drop my life, come to live in a hellhole to spend endless hours watching day television with her? As I observed her carefully, she became sick at the back of the car and Cati had to stop and take her out to breathe some air, treating her with more respect than he had treated me.

There seemed to be something they all feared in my aunty which made them become overly solicitous, and made me feel that everything was crazy.

At the bank, the bank manageress turned out to be a next-generation, well-educated version of the housewife who lived besides my aunt. She was proud, efficient, felt limitless and dangerous because she was powerful and judgemental. A woman with overgrown confidence in her sex and race. She was what the neighbour's daughter, Roberto's wife-to-be, could have aspired to, had she not got herself pregnant and then agreed to marry Roberto.

We sat, my aunt, Cati and myself squashed on a two-seater outside the bank manageress's office, as she made her secretary prepare the papers for the meeting. But the waiting offered me no calmness.

Then the manageress came out herself to welcome my aunt

and ushered her into her office. I followed. My aunt turned to Cati and told him to stay outside; I could tell he was fuming.

The manageress talked only to my aunt during the meeting because she was her client, and my aunt stood dignified for the duration despite the effort this must have physically demanded of her.

The manageress asked my aunt to confirm that I was family. She asked my aunt to confirm that she wanted my name on her account. Next she asked me for my passport, her stare still on my aunt. Holding my passport, the manageress finally glanced at me to acknowledge that I existed. 'You will take care of your aunty,' she said patronisingly.

I nodded, when I wanted to tell her to go fuck herself, but she was holding my passport.

I wanted to tell her that I was only there because my aunt had insisted she wanted me to grab her money the minute she was dead and run, because she could not be bothered to leave a will like every other responsible person would. And that I didn't have the heart to tell my aunt that I would never do such a thing, for reasons too complex for a manageress with a little bird's brain like her to understand. And that I earned this kind of money in a year, frankly, and did not give a shit.

I would have felt justified to act smug, because the manageress was herself acting over-proud and she was only a manageress in a shoddy retail branch in some shitty bank in a lost Cartagena suburb, and was talking to me, a successful international corporate lawyer, as if I were scum. But then I had been useless this whole trip, had I not? Perhaps I was scum. I deserved it.

And all the way through that bank meeting I was not sure. I was not sure about my aunt. I knew Cati, the bank manageress, the neighbours, even my mum and dad could all be happy if I took care of this hot potato, of my aunt's lonely demise. Some of them thought they even had the right to expect it of me. But her? My aunt? I looked at her trying hard to read her in that meeting. She was full of pride. All that effort to live up to who she was. But I really could not guess as to her real wishes and motivations and how she justified herself. And I selfishly concluded she would be happy to die alone, simply reassured in the knowledge that she did not need to worry as to who would end up with her money.

Was that wishful thinking?

That was the deal she had spelt out in her letter.

Was I being unjust to think such a deal possible? Did I care if it wasn't the case? Would I accept any other deal? Would I fight it? Explain to my aunt why any different expectation she may have was unreasonable? Did my aunt's money come with universally recognised responsibilities she didn't need to spell out? Would she really pretend, in my position, I committed to fixing the ailments of an old dying lady, versus returning to attend to my life, to sue for the slightly injured pinkie of an award-winning golfer? Was that a fair exchange?

I was never going to take her money anyway.

I was only letting her think I was, to put her mind at rest! Would anyone believe me?

I got my passport back from the bank manageress and left Cartagena two days after that bank meeting, two endless days in which I visited my aunt at every lunchtime.

I never saw her neighbours again. I never saw Cati even if one of the days was a Wednesday and he should have picked my aunty up to take her to her hairdresser's appointment. I never called Roberto. I took the disrespected jewels with me and never asked my aunt about my grandmother's painting.

I tipped the bellman a final fifty-dollar bill when he got me into the taxi for the airport; I was euphoric.

When I arrived back in London I put the jewels in a drawer, buries under useless papers, double-locked, next to my aunt's chequebook. I would never use anything from her. I planned to forget all about my trip as quickly as I could. I was as disappointed that I had failed to see through her motives, as hurt she had never attempted to understand mine. And I was absolutely embarrassed that I had failed her and perhaps myself.

Still, I also felt that I had bigger fish to fry.

I often thought back to my grandmother's portrait though.

A few months later, September 11 happened.

My partner had unexpectedly been moved to work in Italy and suddenly airports all over the globe were in meltdown. Travel queues were impossible to handle on our schedules. I had to cancel one weekend down to see him, then another. Our relationship felt like it was extinguishing in an agonising manner.

I should have snapped earlier, perhaps after Roberto.

I should have made it brutal.

I had not had it in me though. And I hoped to make it to Milan that week, as I claimed every week, to repair things for good. Until I got Cati's call.

'She's in hospital. She's sick and dying.'

He was breathless.

'They are asking me to authorise a hole to be drilled through her throat.' The news was a bomb hitting me. 'You have to come. And you have to pay. For everything. You have to take care of her. You are the one with the money. I saw how she gave you the chequebook, at the bank.'

Cati would not stop talking, at inhuman speed. And I felt dizzy. I couldn't breathe. Was that how my aunt felt, why she needed a hole? She was dying. I couldn't believe it yet it was hardly unexpected. 'I can't travel there now,' I shouted at Cati to make him stop. I was holding onto the mantelpiece with my phone-free hand as the ceiling of the room circled over my head. 'I have a European trip scheduled for work next week, and with the travel restrictions I may even have to cancel that.' Cati's sudden silence told me he wasn't buying my explanations.

I was a junior, for God's sake. I couldn't cancel work stuff without career consequences. But of course how would he know? And I couldn't disappear from my partner's life or it would be the end of our relationship at such a fragile time; we had been together for over five years, it was not a small thing. Still these all sounded like excuses to me, and surely to Cati.

Most of all, I could not make the decision of whether a hole should be drilled through my aunt's neck. I just couldn't. I felt totally unprepared and without authority, it was too difficult a decision for me who expected one day soon to be able to break big law cases worth millions of dollars. This one thing being asked of me suddenly seemed bigger than any case I had ever been involved in. 'I am happy to sign cheques if you want,' I finally agreed to Cati down the phone. Although I wasn't even happy to do that, handing money to someone I did not trust. But what was the alternative? I didn't want to be involved at all in this affair and wished I had burnt all my aunt had given me before getting on that plane back home that last day in Cartagena. No. I wished that I had never gone to see her, that I had never opened her letter.

Cati hang up.

I didn't sleep that night.

My mum called back early the next morning. They would travel to see my aunt.

My parents stayed in Cartagena for a week, agreed on the breathing tube despite being waved by my aunt out of the room as soon as she saw them. (My mum only told me later.) They arranged for an old people's home to be ready when she came out of hospital. 'Or if,' said the nurse. My mum told me they had nodded. Those days I signed any cheques as per my mother's instructions so that they could sort my aunt's affairs. When they came back, they told me how helpful my aunt's next-door neighbours had been and it felt like a kick in the stomach. 'And Cati,' they added.

I didn't want to talk about it.

My aunt died within weeks of being transferred to the old people's home. I obviously never did anything about the money in her account.

My parents decided to travel back out there. My mum did all the fighting with the authorities regarding my aunt's inheritance, the taxes and the repatriation of the money back to Spain, where my aunt's legal heirs, including my dad, resided. They sold my aunt's house to the daughter of my aunt's neighbours, who had given birth. She had apparently broken her engagement to Roberto and needed all the help she could get, according to her mother, who paid a reduced amount for the flat.

Two-thirds of my aunt's wealth went to my cousins who my aunt deeply disliked, I never understood why. She had not seemed to like me much either I guess, even if she insisted I had always been the destined one. One cousin, the girl, bought a new kitchen. The other took a long round-the-world trip. They had not seen my aunt for thirty years, probably no more than twice in their lives, and they cared about her as much as she had done about them. None of my cousins thanked my mother for her troubles over the inheritance either.

I almost never again wished to talk about my aunt until writing this story, even if they all say I look like her, a boy version. I sometimes dream of her painting of my grandmother, though. I wonder where it is now.

7

Schools panel

Sarah has been invited to a private secondary-schools panel, at the primary prep of her best friend's children. But her friend couldn't come with her in the end.

Sarah doesn't know exactly what to expect.

She has been at a panel once before, a pharmaceutical panel at a big international conference where bland-looking managers stressed over whether big or small was best to drive innovation. She had been extremely bored and left halfway through. But this was when she used to work, nearly nine years ago now, before her marriage. Because almost immediately after her wedding, Sarah got pregnant. Her and her husband mutually decided then his career being time-consuming, she would leave her job. Next, his work had predictively eclipsed their life, but somehow riches hadn't rained upon them the way they had expected, and Sarah had never thought she could afford a posh private secondary school for her baby. Until she had, out of the blue, come into some money following the death of an estranged rich aunt.

My aunt died within weeks of being transferred to the old people's home. I obviously never did anything about the money in her account.

My parents decided to travel back out there. My mum did all the fighting with the authorities regarding my aunt's inheritance, the taxes and the repatriation of the money back to Spain, where my aunt's legal heirs, including my dad, resided. They sold my aunt's house to the daughter of my aunt's neighbours, who had given birth. She had apparently broken her engagement to Roberto and needed all the help she could get, according to her mother, who paid a reduced amount for the flat.

Two-thirds of my aunt's wealth went to my cousins who my aunt deeply disliked, I never understood why. She had not seemed to like me much either I guess, even if she insisted I had always been the destined one. One cousin, the girl, bought a new kitchen. The other took a long round-the-world trip. They had not seen my aunt for thirty years, probably no more than twice in their lives, and they cared about her as much as she had done about them. None of my cousins thanked my mother for her troubles over the inheritance either.

I almost never again wished to talk about my aunt until writing this story, even if they all say I look like her, a boy version. I sometimes dream of her painting of my grandmother, though. I wonder where it is now.

7

Schools panel

Sarah has been invited to a private secondary-schools panel, at the primary prep of her best friend's children. But her friend couldn't come with her in the end.

Sarah doesn't know exactly what to expect.

She has been at a panel once before, a pharmaceutical panel at a big international conference where bland-looking managers stressed over whether big or small was best to drive innovation. She had been extremely bored and left halfway through. But this was when she used to work, nearly nine years ago now, before her marriage. Because almost immediately after her wedding, Sarah got pregnant. Her and her husband mutually decided then his career being time-consuming, she would leave her job. Next, his work had predictively eclipsed their life, but somehow riches hadn't rained upon them the way they had expected, and Sarah had never thought she could afford a posh private secondary school for her baby. Until she had, out of the blue, come into some money following the death of an estranged rich aunt.

Sarah takes a minute to inspect herself in the full-length bathroom mirror. She can hear the babysitter cooking for her daughter, Katia, in the small kitchen down the corridor. Back to the mirror, she thinks she looks ancient despite her recent haircut. At least her new exercise routines keep her a bit more perky, even if they don't seem to be achieving much for her sagging knees. She picks at two unruly hairs over her eyes with shiny tweezers, to tidy up her eyebrows. The shadow above her upper lip seems to have become a permanent facial feature that depresses her, like the clouds over London. Until she decides to stop gazing and squeezes some thick paste rich in minerals out of a dazzling white tiny tube.

Sarah sighs.

The paste hides some damning evidence.

Next she stretches and stretches the slippery skin of her cheeks and around her eyes and forehead using her bony fingers, the way she has been told by her girlfriends. But when she stops pulling and the cream has been well-spread and absorbed, the ravines remain.

Fuck it, she thinks. *Really, fuck it.*

She hears young Tati – short for Tatiana – again, laughing about something with Katia, and suffers a moment of deep jealousy. She has been trying to go for the natural look as of late but today she will put on some make-up. Ten to six, she has time. The invite was six for six twenty, and these things always start late anyway. And Sarah lives only a ten-minute walk away.

After the face paint, she hangs some pearls on her neck, giraffing away to hide any drooping, then changes her mind for a simpler golden chain. *Pearls with beige mid-heels shout middle age!*

As Sarah enters the kitchen she is struck by the intoxicating smell of garlic. It almost hurts her eyes. She could never feed Katia this much garlic but the girl seems to happily take it from Tati. Does garlic keep Tati looking young?

No. She *is* young.

Tati leaves whatever she's doing and claps her hands admiringly, as if congratulating Sarah on dressing up, going out. *She's such a child*, Sarah thinks. Tati thinks her madam looks wonderful.

'Will you see Coco there tonight, Mum?' Katia asks, enquiring after the older daughter of Sarah's friend.

'It's adults only, boring stuff.' To tell the truth, Sarah would rather take Katia with her. She hates leaving her with Tati, even if she trusts Tati to keep her safe. But it's just she knows she will have Katia watching trash TV whilst she busies herself ironing, trying to be helpful. Of course, it's an efficient use of Tati's time and Sarah's money but... perhaps not the best for the girl? In any case, it will only be for a few hours.

'Will you see Nunu there?' Katia asks again.

Sarah wonders why all girls have to be called funny names nowadays. Nunu is a friend of Coco, one of the twins of Orla, married to... She doesn't remember and hopes it's not Alzheimer's. They all bonded at Coco's birthday party two weeks ago, one her husband naturally forgot to put in his diary.

'She won't be there either,' says Sarah.

'You know we call their school Pretty Horse Poo.' Katia laughs out hard and Tati joins. 'For PHP,' the girl clarifies, Prima-Rose

Hill Preparatory.

Sarah laughs too.

'Mums there look so pretty,' Katia adds and Sarah doesn't laugh anymore. She kisses her daughter on the forehead and leaves down the corridor.

'You smell of roses,' the girl shouts after her.

'I will be a couple of hours.' Sarah smiles and waves at Tati and Katia as she walks towards her front door.

On Sarah's walk to school it's still light, although a bit nippy for the time of the year.

The sunlight this evening is almost that of childhood afternoons, she takes a minute to enjoy before regret returns. *Time passes and suddenly life takes us.* She glances at funny-shaped clouds above her head.

The Spanish bakers on her way are still open and the waitress salutes Sarah through her window. They grind her so hard, Sarah wonders how will she survive if she ever has children. She knows the waitress is great with children. She had her babysit Katia once, and Katia talked about their dreamt fairytales for days: 'Once upon a time, there was a youthful beautiful princess with a magic unicorn...'

Next, Sarah strolls past the Turkish kebab house where the Iranian owner blows her a kiss. She ate there a lot a few months ago, when she had felt particularly lonely, and not only because the meat was decent and the man balanced the spices to perfection. But also for the conversation. Amir had gifted her and Katia half a watermelon back then, because Katia had been wanting and Sarah couldn't find one in the market. And a friendship had grown from that. Katia constantly laughed that theirs was a watermelon friendship, totally oblivious to any other non-fruit-related feeling that could have flourished between her mother and this similarly lonely man.

Before turning into PHP's street, a pigeon fails to get out of Sarah's way, remaining seated on the centre of the pavement. When she mock-kicks it, nothing happens.
Perhaps the bird is hurt.
She knows she should sense pity but doesn't. She finds pigeons disgusting even if she feels guilty she should not be that cruel to a living thing. She prefers to walk away quickly not to have to look at the bird, and in doing so, she nearly slips over a puddle of oil, perhaps from a delivery van or a moped.
Bloody dangerous!
But at least she has averted a fall, which would have been catastrophic, surely soiling her clothes and making her cancel the whole evening. That's if she had not broken a leg! Sarah knows she can't break a leg.
Who would take care of Katia?

At the gates of the school Sarah buzzes twice.
There seem to be plenty of doors to buzz at after the main entrance too, and she's startled by the level of security. But she knows one cannot blame the school given how things stand in the world nowadays. Only three weeks ago, she read about a worrying incident near their tube station, two minutes down the

road, where a middle-aged man had tried to force a twelve-year-old girl into his car. The girl hadn't been from her daughter's school or from PHP, but it went to show the world was wretched. The thought brings a chill up Sarah's spine as she strolls into her friend's posh school.

Will she ever be able to let Katia go?

What will happen the day the girl insists on walking to school on her own?

How will she ever build the courage to let her girl grow up?

Tougher tests are awaiting, which Sarah doesn't want to think of, not know. Perhaps she should allow her husband to send Katia boarding at eleven and get rid of all her weaknesses in one go; the hard way. But she did not even have the heart to let Katia off for that full week with the Browns in Cornwall last summer. She reduced her daughter's trip to two days and worried every single hour of them. *Life ahead seems paved with hell,* she stresses as she thinks about her Katia. *Stop it!* She immediately tells herself. She better be thinking of how to explain her presence in a school her daughter doesn't attend, for starters. Her friend's name should suffice?

Sarah is thinking all these thoughts when someone looking like a sixty-year-old Inès de La Fressange opens the last door to the school building proper, and offers her a welcoming hand. She directs Sarah to sign in and bring herself down a set of coloured stairs to the auditorium.

There, a long table lined with wine bottles and glasses tinted in various shades awaits. Directly behind the table, Sarah quickly counts up to ten rows of chairs on either side of a narrow passage leading to the panelists' stage with four chairs. The room smells to her, of something like petrol.

At the drinks table, a petite-looking woman, elegant but more of an elderly Harry Potter than a glamorous model this time, shakes Sarah's hand briskly, then immediately frees her to her own devices before Sarah has time to explain who she is. She had worried for nothing.

Some people have already helped themselves to wine and many of the bottles on the table are half-empty. Most guests, about three-quarters of whom are women, are now seated. Sarah thinks the women look a tad stylish but not stylish enough to let anyone think that they dressed for the occasion, like she has. Perhaps she should have come before and mingled over wine ahead of the talk but she's no good at mingling. And she sees Katia was right that the mothers in this school look prettier than average, which intimidates her.

Other than the first two rows, the auditorium is quite packed. In any case, Sarah has forgotten her glasses so she strolls down the aisle to the front as dignified as she can on her wobbly heels, and sits on the second row, she has no choice, by a mum she recognises from Coco's birthday party. She remembers the woman being nice enough, perhaps not as scary as some of the other mums.

Sarah says hello.

She has left a seat free between them on her right and a few empty seats to her left near the aisle.

'Cassandra,' the woman offers Sarah her hand.

'Sarah, Katia's mum, from Coco's party,' Sarah offers an explanation that they already know each other.

Cassandra nods, trying to remember. 'It should be interesting tonight,' she says. 'We need some tips to cut down our list of applications for Lili.'

Sarah sighs deep.

Nunu, Coco, Lili… all the same rhythm to them.

She has no list of school application choices for Katia as of yet. On stage, three men, indistinguishably solemn and bald, and a woman with a bright red jacket sit on their chairs.

As the auditorium doors are closed and everyone awaits the start of the event, Nunu's mum, Orla, rushes down the aisle holding a glass wine, to sit on Sarah's left. She's dragging a young man behind her.

'Orla,' she says offering Sarah a hand. Then she recognises it's her. 'You are Katia's mum.'

Sarah stretches her hand to Orla's.

'Did not know your girl is at PHP?'

Cassandra on Sarah's right side looks confused at Orla's question, and Sarah feels the need to offer clarification to them both, despite the headmistress, the Harry Potter lookalike lady, having started her introduction for the panel. 'Cecilia, Coco's mum, invited me. She couldn't attend herself.'

Orla smiles and nods. She does not think much of Coco's mum, who smells of a family fortune come with country estate for her to sport her wellies on weekends, and stride about the ancient grounds riding pretty horses.

'I am interested for Katia,' Sarah adds, crossing her right beige shoe to rub behind her left ankle. Then she stops jiggling it almost immediately, not to damage her expensive stockings. She's embarrassed.

'Great schools here today,' Orla cheers, 'although half are boys-only.'

Looking at Orla's glass of wine, Sarah impulsively yearns for one herself. She feels unexpectedly hot and takes her jacket off. She wants to rally the courage to walk up to the drinks table, but the whole shebang has kicked off. Orla and the young man beside her toast their glasses. *What to?* Sarah wonders.

What to? Cassandra ponders. She has been looking at the couple suspiciously across Sarah, as if they were the kind of people to buy your organs then make your death relatively nice for you. And Sarah suddenly remembers how Cecilia had warned her. That Cassandra was a bit of an old cow and a gossiper. And that Orla was more interested in sexual freedom than the sanctity of matrimony, a comment Sarah had felt totally out of order, even if whispered, at a child's birthday party.

'To the future,' Orla has murmured to her companion.

Sarah hesitates for a second whether the man by Orla is the same she was with at Coco's birthday party. She thinks he's not. He's not Orla's husband. He's not Nunu's father. Cassandra catches Sarah looking at Orla's man and flickers with disapproval.

The woman on stage in the red jacket is from Wimbledon High House, one of the best schools in London. 'Girls-only,' she warns parents in her crisp introduction.

Orla nods to Sarah. 'She's brilliant,' about Wimbledon High House's headmistress. Apparently, Orla has met her before, seems much more knowledgeable about secondary schools than Sarah is; *She has done her homework,* Sarah thinks.

Sarah has not.

Well, Katia is only in year three. But so are Coco and Nunu and their mums seem all over their secondary-school choices already. *Still, there's time, is there not?* Sarah tells herself she should stop fretting. She should have grabbed that drink. The petrol smell keeps annoying her.

The bald panelist on the far right, the only one wearing a tie, is the first to get serious air time. But someone very tall has rushed in to sit in front of Sarah, in the first row, and she suddenly can't see the speakers' heads anymore.

'You have decisions to make,' the speaker tells the anxious parents in the audience.

There is eerie silence.

'Day or boarding. Co-ed or single-sex.'

Sarah listens to the man's preaching. Life or death, she expects him to say next. She feels daunted again. Next Orla's man besides her squeezes Orla's hand and Sarah sees Cassandra throwing them another look.

Sarah's now absolutely positive, Orla's husband at Coco's looked different. He was a different man. Cassandra's constant spying and her grimaces thrown their way seem to confirm that. Perhaps it's Orla's brother, considers Sarah, and siblings squeeze hands tenderly in their family. Or maybe Orla came by some terrible news this past week and needs her hand squeezed by a friend whilst her husband is travelling, although she does look pretty cheery, not at all preoccupied by any sad news.

Orla is aware of the two mums in her same row watching her companion's every move and feels a mixture of pride, rage and pity. She bends to leave her glass of wine on the floor by Sarah's feet for a moment, and crosses Sarah's stare on her way up. Next, she smoothes her skirt. Butterflies.

More feminine than usual, Sarah thinks of Orla's skirt as she recalls her almost uniformed like a traffic warden at Coco's party. She never thought of Orla as the feminine type, proud of showing her contours, and Coco's party is not the only occasion she has to judge by. They have coincided before and Orla has always worn a careless tomboy look. Nothing wrong with that. Orla was the one who inspired Sarah's own hair cut.

Cassandra on Sarah's other side is fuming. *School events are not the right place to play out silly romances.* She thinks it's ridiculous. *How desperate can Orla be?* Sarah increasingly feels between two sides of an olive presser, even if she can't entirely grasp the motives for Cassandra's hate. She takes a pencil and little Moleskine out of her jacket pocket, to hide behind it.

'Is that not a bit too keen?' Cassandra throws an unexpected ditch at her and she closes her notebook immediately.

Just when the man next to Orla starts stroking Orla's thigh. *In public!* thinks Cassandra. *It's outrageous. At her own daughter's school!* Cassandra's spleen is about to rip.

Orla knows, to right-thinking people she may seem a mindless whore. And come to think of it, she has never felt more at ease than with whores. She's aware her actions could be tried and found wanting. Why not approved and granted benchmark status instead? She could not care less either way, really. She calmly sips her wine as one of the matching bald panelists on stage, the one with the tie still, caresses his checkered neckwear at length, explaining gravely why girls and boys are different, 'It is good for boys to be boys growing up in a boys-only school,' he sounds the kind of headmaster running an old-fashioned British den with manservants rather than an international club where fashionable oligarchs' offspring and dictators' sons are sent to acquire some English polish, at their leisure.

Sarah sighs, still only able to see the back of someone's head in front of her; his neck skin scaly, like a ninety-year-old's. She glances to the side for a rest, to see Orla's man collecting their two empty glasses, presumably heading for a second round, and feels like asking him to get her one too. *With some nibbles on the side, even if they were sad-looking.* It will save her from having to cook dinner alone when she gets back home.

But she doesn't dare ask.

Cassandra sends Orla's companion yet another furtive glance as he gets up, thinking to herself, *What a cheek. This man is not even a parent of the school, a dad to Orla's children and he's drinking our wine. At least it's bad wine!* she knows. Cassandra's a member of the parents' association and she bought the wine. 'Poor Charles,' she whisper in Sarah's ear sparking a eureka moment.

Sarah has remembered the name of Orla's husband: Charles.

Out of the blue, she remembers everything about Charles. Charles definitely does not look at all like this man next to Orla. Charles talked a lot. Very amicable. Without serious virtue or vice, other than his drinking? A vice in common with this other man? Charles would have said hello to her though. *And he had a Scottish accent?* Yes, Sarah remembers now. And the more she remembers, the more confused she looks. And Cassandra frowns at her confusion. But Orla is a rock next to them, until her man arrives with two fresh wine glasses and sits back next to her. A bald boring man is still talking on stage, perhaps the one with the tie or one of the other two who look the same.

Sarah is distracted though. She decides Orla has gone for a different type. *Can't blame her!* she thinks, *She was always bitching about her husband even if he seemed great, complained he was around too much when she would have preferred him away.* Perhaps Orla held a fear her husband kept her too close, that he could once grow into the one person who would know everything about her? But Sarah can swear they were still together two weeks ago. At Coco's birthday party.

The voice of the woman speaker emerges by surprise from the stage.

'Welcome!' exclaims Orla, who, like Sarah, has had enough of the nobility and pomposity heard so far from the bald, male side of the podium (even if she was hardly listening after a while). 'Bored me more than a step-by-step bullying workshop!' she adds.

'Another huge decision, 11+ or 13+,' the headmistress in the red jacket speaks.

Sarah still can't see her, but her voice at least claims less righteousness than that of the earlier male speakers, until she informs the audience her school does not do 13+, so if their kid is not ready at eleven they can forget it, as if latecomers could expect to be disinherited. *Will Katia be ready at eleven?* Sarah's brain machinations kick in again. She thinks all this mental activity is crazy because this was supposed to be a relaxing evening.

Cassandra glances at Orla once more, checking what she's getting up to with her man. When Orla smiles, she offers her thumbs up back to her. But none of them buy it, of course. Cassandra is getting increasingly upset, until she eventually works herself indignant, that her own husband is not by her. Another late night at the office. It's a small computer game company but he works directly with the CEO. And they are releasing results the next day, even if they are a private company. But they are releasing them to their major investor so it's big news. Cassandra doesn't know why. Doesn't understand. Does not want to understand anymore. At least, he brought a nice specialty Lego from his last trip to California for the girls. Lego is from Denmark but this is another Lego of course; a cool one from Silicon Valley. Cassandra always hated Lego anyway. Did her husband notice her little attempts to make the place nicer whilst he was gone? He has even stopped taking Lili climbing on Sundays, because the younger sibling asked to come too and he can't cope. He is just not a kiddies' dad. How can you be a child-unfriendly dad? Of course you can. It's quite normal. Cassandra's vexed though. *He should be here, hearing about schools.* But he leaves it all to her. It would just be nice to have his hand on her thigh, perhaps.

The woman in the red jacket swears she knows every single girl in her school, personally. Yes. Their personalities, what they are up to... 'They are wonderful girls,' she says.

If Katia ends up going to the Wimbledon school, the woman will get to know her better than her own dad, thinks Sarah. She is back taking notes. She likes the woman and her red jacket. And the man in front of Sarah has moved slightly so she can almost see the speakers' faces too. *My daughter needs to be inspired by strong women like this one in her red jacket,* she thinks. And Sarah suddenly wishes she had been a civil engineer and could take Katia round town, pointing out all the great buildings she had built. *Concrete evidence of greatness, this is what Katia needs. Pardon the pun on the concrete,* Sarah smiles to herself.

Orla, in an energetic resolution, is now cupping her hand over her man's, both having finished their second glass of wine, and Sarah feels a flare of embarrassment over them as she imagines their silent conversation: 'Lick me. I am licking. I am leaking. Lick me. Lick my lick. Lick my leak.' She doesn't know where her thoughts come from but she senses so much intimacy to them, his hand's blood flowing into Orla's groin. *These two don't want to change for anything or anyone!* Sarah doesn't dare look at Cassandra, whose phone suddenly rings thankfully offering her a way out.

Orla reflects to the mess of her life these last few months... But now there is a tiny bit of hope.

Though it worries her that her girls have been too resilient, as if they did not care much. And she feels guilty her ex, Charles, has been so adamant about putting the kids first. 'Let you be with this other person just as long as I can see the children. I will live next door,' he has promised and delivered. 'I will cause no fuss.' He has even delivered on that. Charles must see her with her new man every day, through his bay window facing hers. *It must be excruciating, yet he does not flinch,* Orla thinks. The kids don't complain either. Everyone gets on and it makes her feel terrible that she has created all this havoc they refuse to react to, for her own pleasure. She might as well enjoy her pleasure now, that feeling of growth like she hadn't felt for a long time. But she wishes everyone around her could grow too.

She squeezes the hand of her man even tighter and he smiles fondly at her.

Question time. A mum puts her hand up and asks the panelists about private tuition.

Cassandra is back in her seat.

Sarah feels bad she has never arranged any for Katia. She doesn't even know what exactly the mum is referring to. She feels stupid. How could she think she would be good enough to teach her child herself? Cassandra can identify the terror on Sarah's face. 'You have someone? I can give you a good number later.' *What's a good number? What will it cost?* Sarah puts on a thankful face.

One of the bald panelists takes the question, urging the parents not to bother prepping their children for entrance school exams because it will do no good.

Orla nods left of Sarah and Sarah is relieved.

Cassandra frowns on Sarah's right, as if the panelist was talking bullshit.

Sarah looks at her notes again. Single-sex or co-ed. Boarding or day. 11+ or 13+. Surrounded by what looks like doodles in the shape of cocks whilst she was really only drawing lucky *peperoncini* charms. Two of the schools in the panel are boys-only and the co-ed one is too far from London. Sarah's heart could not have Katia boarding. So it's the woman in red if anything. Her first choice from today, Sarah's only choice. She has not learnt much from the event really, and she starts to feel nauseated again by the silent flow between Orla and Cassandra against the background of petrol smell. *Poor Charles!* She wants to go now; this was not a good evening.

But the speakers are still talking, one of the bald men again, she can't tell which as they all even have the same voice, advising not to troll your children around too many schools which seems to be irritating Cassandra. He assures it's best to aim for three choices: aspirational, first choice and fall-out. 'Somehow three is always the number,' Cassandra complains to Sarah. And five rows behind, a mum with her arm up is howling, 'Best way to choose?' A different bald speaker, the one without a tie but with a bow and a slightly acuter tone of voice, tells her there is some kind of holy grail, a Bible of posh private schools. Sarah tries to note the name of the book down but has missed it, the best piece of info she could have got tonight! She doesn't have the bravery to ask Orla or Cassandra to tell her.

Will the speaker repeat the name of the reference text perhaps?

But he's returned to the subject of tutoring, agreeing with previous panelists on its uselessness and boasting endless made-up evidence like some asshole from McKinsey (perhaps any of her husband's colleagues), 'Buy a pack in WHSmith on verbal, non-verbal and reasoning and save on tutoring.' He sounds assertive, perhaps he's long WHSmith shares.

'Bollocks to that!' Cassandra whispers.

Her language takes Sarah by surprise.

An elegant lady with black bouffant hair has just arrived, very late, and is marching down the aisle to sit in the first row, on the left side of the room.

Sarah recognises her.

She's Ilaria's mum from Katia's old nursery. Sarah didn't know she sent her kids to PHP. She remembers her with her husband, a marketing power couple. They had once joined Sarah and her husband on a golf weekend years ago, and they had very much enjoyed each other's company. In fact, Sarah is now certain she saw Ilaria's father too as she came in, sitting at the back of the auditorium. But she was not sure it was him. *Of course it is him. It must be.* He was alone though. He did not say hello.

Ilaria's mum asks a question, despite having arrived late and missed the panel. Sarah looks at Ilaria's mum then back at her husband she has spotted once again in the back row.

Cassandra notices Sarah's back and forth, 'They have been separated for three months but still attend everything together, for the children,' she tells Sarah.

Sarah's heart misses a beat. 'They could not be further apart, on opposite sides of the floor,' she was not meant to express her thought aloud.

'At least she has left her new boyfriend in the car,' comes down Cassandra's chainsaw. She's staring at Orla.

Ten minutes later, Sarah leaves the evening deflated.

She stops at the Iranian on the way home. 'In for a kebab,' she tells Amir. 'Minced lamb, please. You know the way I like it. And

a chat,' she admits.
Amir is so nice to her.
As she sucks his meat listening to his stories, she imagines them running away together. They could buy a little house in Turkey, with her money for Katia's secondary school, on the coast, somewhere like Gümüşlük in the Bodrum peninsula. Open a tiny restaurant there for mezzes and grilled fish. Such a better life. Better weather. Better use of her money. Sarah knows she could definitely do without fancy company, expensive clothes and chic restaurants, if only she had some love. Anyway, all marriages are doomed. Has she not seen it tonight? The system is broken. But how would she explain it to Katia?
She can't.
We must follow a formula, if anything to give a frontage to the void, she knows she's wrong though. But still she gets up and kisses Amir, who presses his body against hers passionately for a moment because she reminds him of his wife who passed away last year. He thanks Allah's goodness that they had never had children or he could not cope.
And after, Sarah goes back home, to Katia, promising Amir she will come back to see him more often.

8

Drunk

Hold on to your glass and let me decant some favourite blunders...

I woke up with the light, in the middle of a golf course, being drizzled on. Was I in my ball gown? Turquoise. I remembered a party; a flash of a boy raced in and out of one of my brain's compartments. I could recall his voice: 'Hole number nine. It's a fucker. Have not managed to take it right yet. It fails me every time.' Had it failed him last night too?

I tried to stand up.

My stomach was in a knot and my head circled a little. I still had my knickers on and there was no vomit down my dress; these were all good signs.

I checked my watch. It was before six.

I hoped grandma had not yet realised I was missing. I would not want her to worry about me. She had known I was out for a blast but would soon find all my cousins had made it back. Or had they? No way to know.

I looked around.

I had no fucking idea where I was. Everything was green grass around me... Well, of course; it was a golf course.

I quickly assessed I had two options. Did I remember where I had come from? If so, I could walk that same way back until I hit the club house. What if someone was still up there? Waiters? Cleaners? Management? Guests? How embarrassing... I would just walk past, my head high. What if there was nobody and the main gates out were locked? In any case, I did not remember where I had come from.

Option two: the ocean. I could see the ocean from where I was barely standing. I could head to the beach and jump the barriers. They were low. Once on the beach I knew my way home. Option two was granted.

As I walked towards the sea I did two things.

I went through how much worse things could have been in my mind. What if I had woken up being knocked by a golf ball on my head? What if the players had been my uncles? What if I hadn't woken up at all? Enough. I thanked God I looked decent despite whatever had happened during the night. And despite the hangover. At least I wasn't dripping with semen although that didn't mean much.

After thanking God for the worst not having happened, I started to try to put the pieces back together to investigate what had actually happened. The boy had been the cool one with the baby Jesus yellow locks and the expensive tailored suit everyone seemed to know the brand of. He was from Bilbao, from one of a handful of regal families. He had professed to be unattached according to my last conversation I could remember at the bar over a triple gin and tonic with my cousin. I was suddenly sorry I may have let him down, the boy. I had been devouring him at his beach cabin next to us all summer, dreaming of what I could do to him. All the girls had, like cats in heat with hallucinations.

Unexpectedly, I reprimanded myself. 'Fucking hell, Cristina, he left you there! Paralytic in the middle of a golf course.' All that surname, and the suit and the looks but where were his bloody manners! Could aristocracy get away with no manners at all? It was ludicrous. They dreamed a plutocracy but were all a bunch of yokels! All I remembered was a kiss and then falling back onto the lawn. I did not remember getting back up. Had he left me there and rejoined the party in search of another victim? (I would have to modify a curling iron and burn the whole episode out of my brain! like I had read in a recent novel of a woman who had been triple-fucked by her boyfriend in different orifices; she had not enjoyed it in the slightest and it had changed her feelings for him.) And how had we got to the golf course in the first place? Would we not get in trouble for walking through the grass, me in my high heels? Where were my heels?

Shit! Too late.

I was halfway to the beach without any shoes and I didn't remember seeing them around hole nine. I would tell Granny I had given them to some other irresponsible cousin who had lost hers so she could get back home unharmed. And Granny would believe me.

A surname came to mind out of the blue.

'Abaitua!' I cried to the sky above the golf course.

My dad had talked about them ahead of the party. He had said they were good people, even if they were from Bilbao. Clever, too; you could trust them to make you answer your own question when you asked them something, Dad had convincingly advised a room full of family as if he was trained in manipulating thought.

'*Me cago en tu puta madre!*' I cried again to the sky, clear as it hardly ever is in that region of Spain. Yes, I shat on Abaitua's whore mother. It was the least I could do.

The golf club's party was the highlight of the summer. Would my extended family down to my uncles and aunties, cousins, second cousins, friends and acquaintances have been proud of me had I made it with an Abaitua? We would never know because I had clearly fallen short. Would they be disappointed?

'There had been much drink,' I would tell them. These days there was always too much to drink and I seemed to drink it all...

We were young. Our livers were strong or we just didn't give a fuck about them, or both. That party the night before had been sold as the pinnacle of summer parties. Not that it totally justified me drinking until I passed out but kind of. Our parents had even taken a photo of all the girl cousins dressed for the occasion and encouraged us, told us we looked wonderful. 'Go eat the world!' their smiles had urged us. 'Go get the rich boys!' Even if they are bound one day soon to become paunchy, bald, middle-aged, corrupt laughers at multimillion dollar fines for taking risks that kill people! We were too happy not to ask how they made their money. And in turn they were more well-practised than anyone in window dressing, of course.

Our male cousins hadn't been there to protect us. They hadn't wanted to come. There were that sort of males in our family, males that didn't like golf club parties until they were older or maybe never. In any case, in such civilised company, what would we have needed protection from!

When I reached the beach, I looked for a tear in the flimsy wooden planks delimiting the course and slid through, out of the golfing area into the sand, not without waving to hole nine in the distance. I had not even needed to climb the wall.

Two nights later. The Abaitua king had seen and ignored me at the beach but I wasn't deflated. The surfers had finally landed in town ahead of a world championship, the reason for which I had been learning surfers' speak most of the summer; I would rebound.

There were only two weeks left before going back to school in London and I needed to make the best of them to compete with accounts of: Indian chants and grass-smoking in the Himalayas; Ironman in Lanzarote after rowing the full length of the Thames; strangers in dark rooms in Madrid and bulls in Pamplona; mud-fighting cum martini-swimming in weird music festivals across southern England (or Ibiza); and 'do your thing' at Edinburgh Fringe. Anything went and a few romantically coloured friendships were always a must amongst my capital-based fellow students during summer.

A spot of bad luck meant the surfers camping in my home town that year looked mostly like dirty monkeys and nobody took my fancy. Even my cousins agreed. Even Cuca who had never been particularly picky when it came to surfers. So I went for plan B, or what I called the home plan, because one always needs a plan one can ultimately fall back to; like a comfort zone.

There was a waiter, a few years older than me, curly hair, no glasses, a tad pudgy despite the weekend sit-ups and the bike, in a bar. His bike fetish was a secret from his co-workers but all I got.

He had been after me the whole summer in tree-frog courtship mode, and I could never repay him the amount of drinks he had gifted me. Except perhaps I could, in a way... Game, set, match. I convinced my cousins to go to his bar on that night, two nights after hole nine. In any case, it was *the* bar. Everyone went to that bar. Or if not that bar the one next to it or the one next to that. Because there was really only one street in town and there were only three bars.

In the bar, the waiter welcomed and served us, and smiled to me, specifically. And somehow because he was clever, a graduate at uni and only waitering during the vacation to pay fees, he knew that that night was *the night*. So after three drinks precisely, when I was starting to get in the mood, in a very unusual gesture he stopped offering. He said he didn't want me to be drunk when he would walk me home, 'for a quickie back on the porch' I added then claimed not to know what I had meant.

I did exactly know what I had meant but his effort to control me, even if it was to look after me, had suddenly pissed me off. And I bought a fourth and a fifth and a sixth drink myself to spite him, to make sure I would be drunk when he walked me home.

Down the *malecón* with him, his friend and one of my cousins – because it had obviously turned into a double date – I realised my legs were failing me. I tried to walk by the edge next to the beach where the high tide made the waves break against the promenade, so that at least the refreshing splash would help me hold myself together; I wasn't walking straight.

At one point, I must have fallen to the floor.

I realised one of my knees was bleeding and staining my skirt.

This is when he told me off. The waiter turned to me and told me that I drank too much. We were alone by then. My cousin had obviously been snatched to a private corner down the beach or under a portico by the waiter's gentleman friend.

'He's not my friend,' he said. 'He only works with me.'

'Well, I will bloody blame you if anything happens to her,' I said in an accusatory tone.

'You are such a nice girl. Why do you have to always get so drunk? You need to take care of yourself. Look at your knee.' He looked at me with pity.

God, I had gifted myself the type of man who read you the rules book, chapter and verse, while you were glumly. 'That is so fucking rich of you. Who the fuck do you think you are?' I asked him. But I could see it in his eyes that he meant to be caring. 'I am not fucking drunk anyway and I'm going to prove it.'

That's when I jumped.

I jumped into the sea.

I must have thought I risked nothing more than I could reading a book at the library; perhaps a papercut? All I remember next is thinking that I had misjudged. The next wave arrived with unexpected force and Batman wasn't coming to save my ass. I thought the tide was going to crash me against the cement of the *malecón*. But the waiter jumped in time and took me out. He saved me from being drowned fully clothed along with the contents of my skirt's pockets!

We sat soaked on the bench.

I looked tragic but claimed it wasn't my fault: it's never a tragic figure's fault – that's what makes her tragic. A group of youngsters passed by and laughed at us. At me. It was five in the morning and they were probably as drunk as I was, but they had not thrown themselves into the sea from the *malecón*.

When the waiter recovered his breath, he looked at me in disgust. I had lost my shoes again. But at least my knee had stopped bleeding. He got up and walked away. I sat there, thinking of what excuse I would tell my grandma to explain the wet clothes. Perhaps I would just leave them on the pile for the washing and hope for the best.

Two days later. My grandmother had given me something to take to my uncle at San Francisco's parish downtown; he was a priest.

As I headed for the back door of the church, I heard some muffled sounds. Then I turned and saw her, slouched in a weird position trying to hold her back up against the corner whilst her limp legs drooped over the floor. Her face seemed contorting. Everywhere else she was lifeless. Her hair was dirty. Her jeans here unbuttoned and I could see her silvery knickers. Her arms were bare and full of scratches and pricks. Under her loose sleeveless T-shirt she wore nothing and it was so transparent I could distinguish the areolas round her breasts. I still remember her dark hard nipples to this day. I thought in another body or at another time they may have looked beautiful.

She was holding a bottle.

She was a limp thing all over but her right fingers were all scrunched, hanging on to her vodka bottle, a prized possession. Her hand looked in pain but she didn't shift her fingers. Her sight, in my uncle's church, scared the hell out of me; almost enough to adopt a distaste for religion. There was nothing in her eyes; a kind of void like the world was emptying out. For a minute I saw myself in this young woman, in that void, and wanted to run.

I only ran inside to call my uncle.
'Not the Urrutia girl again,' he said.
'She looks young. She's a drug-user. She's homeless, I am sure.' I couldn't stop talking from the fright.
My uncle came out. 'It's the Urrutia girl, *pobre chiquilla*.' Poor one. 'It all starts with a few drinks and then more drinks and then drugs and… They let her go astray.' My uncle frowned, took her in his arms and carried her inside.

On my way home I kept thinking of that name.
The Urrutia girl. She had been my age. She could have been me. I had heard that name before. And then it came back. The Urrutias and the Abaituas. That's where I had heard it before. I shivered and promised God I wouldn't over-drink ever again.

9

New face

The first thing you notice is a large picture of a tiger, a bit like *Whistlejacket* by Stubbs in the National Gallery but a more exotic twin. It faces a full-length mirror covering the front wall. In the five metres between the painting and the mirror, there is a top-quality Cadillac full trapeze glowing like an instrument of torture, a less intimidating reformer which could pass for a spartan single bed, and a barrel. Not a wine barrel, of course.

Perhaps I like to torture myself.

Nobody pays me to do so. In fact, I get paid to inflict good pain on other people, whether in person or virtually. Everything is payable on my website.

At ten, noon and two, when school mums are at their quietest, I open my doors to them. I lay out fresh flowers and light-scented candles in the relaxation area, and ring my Buddhist chimes. I welcome them one by one: by appointment only. They dislike being late yet invariably are. Reschedules are easy though, for an extra fee. I'm always only a click away.

My oasis of wellness also features a recliner, a sink, and no window with a view of any kind. What is there to see somewhere as grubby as Portobello? In any case, I am no believer in Pilates with a view: by the ocean, by the lake… My mums come to me for the torment, not scenery. Most of all, they come to save their face.

Putri shines my oak floors every morning, in her little maid's outfit. She is petite with Asian features and straight long black hair in a tight bun, and she's very efficient. The studio side walls hold wood panels hiding different sets of doors; she shines those too. I myself water my Bonsai over the mantelpiece. Putri and I carry out all these tasks precisely between nine and nine thirty every weekday.

Next, after I have ushered Putri out and shut the studio doors to my house, but before I open my second set of doors to the mums waiting in the courtyard, I choose the day's invigorate bra and tights of functional microfiber, and sit for ten minutes on a stool in front of the front wall mirror; if I feel in a good mood I let my cat, Joseph, as in Joseph Pilates, stay with me. It is my own facial fitness time, time to look at my face before facing the world.

Today there is nobody in the courtyard when I open the doors wide, so I close them again. I fetch a pair of neon running shoes from a hidden wardrobe, the pink pair, throw a grey sweater over my bra, the one I bought during my last trip to D.C. when I went for my masters reunion, blow out the candles in the welcome area and briskly stroll out in the direction of the coffee shop. I feel my chestnut ponytail dangling over my back. Fuck! It's raining again. My hood comes in handy.

I cross the road to the shop. Three old men are sitting outside, enjoying their coffees under the rain. They all look like ex-alcoholics. They seem weirdly calm when they lift their hands in unison to say hi to me. I walk in and join the queue by the bar, immediately scanning for any potential clients; it's a habit.

It takes a minute to locate two mums. One is standing by the side wall, stuffing a chocolate croissant down her gob in a flash, hoping she's transparent and that nobody will report her. She wears a baggy black sweater to hide how overweight she is. The other one has just asked for a tall non-fat latte with caramel drizzle. She's hoping to get in her new bikini in time for her Caribbean holiday at half-term but it will be a stretch. There are all sorts of ways in which these women could flourish as they grow old. But do they deserve it? At the moment they are clueless.

Then, unexpectedly, she comes to me like a puma approaching her prey out of nowhere, like my painted tiger.

'Are you Esperanza?'

I'm taken aback. That's my old name. Nobody calls me by that name anymore. Nobody would recognise my face who could remember that was my old name. But she has, 'Jo? From Salomons?' We had joined the same year and attended the training programme together. It had been 1997.

My husband.

He stays in a white room in the Harley Psychiatric Institute in London. There is one such institute, even if they try to keep it secret. Like my room of pain, my husband's white room has no windows. He has been there for five years. It was the summer I changed my face. When I returned from Mount Koya, back to my new studio he had helped design and fully financed for me in our own house. He saw my new face and checked out. My husband voluntarily checked out of our home. Our kids were in boarding school because courses had already started.

That autumn, I launched my services under the EspeCarma brand name. It was hardly a requirement to avoid destitution, as I retained access to the little fortune my husband had amassed before he abruptly retired. He hasn't so far made any claim to it from his room at the Harley Psychiatric Institute. He has only asked, by letter, that I please pay his rent there. And after five years, we are both well settled and belong to our places; him to his immaculate white bed and walls, tray foods and pill schedules (no dinners replete with silver candelabra and tons of glistening glazed ham with pineapple! even if it's Harley Street); me to my new face, my machines of torture, Joseph the cat, loyal old Putri, candles and chimes. Our children do not belong to any of these two places but don't need to visit anymore; they are enjoying university, growing up in the belief they'll see a better world. When anyone who knew my husband asks, I joke that I have had him buried under the floorboards.

Jo in front of me belongs to the world before my husband, to the world with my old face. She acknowledges I have changed.

'You look wonderful,' she says, full of bad surprise.

'It's all natural,' I promise her and invite her for a coffee. We sit at a table at the back and time-travel.

It never seemed that bad back then. We worked very hard. We played very hard. Different bosses were always around.

Different male colleagues were always around and we never ceased to compete, me and Jo. There had been Media and there had been Pharma, and I had got what I wanted; Jo had taken what was left. Then there had been Fabio and there had been Arnaud, and I had chased both just to irritate Jo, even if I didn't really like either of them deep down. But she had really wanted Fabio and had got him in the end. They had married and churned out kids. Then one day after six years, in late spring, I had come to work and they told me Jo had left. Just like that.

I long wandered what had happened, but the two times I had seen her years after she left, I had been too busy bragging about my own life, the life with my husband when I still had him. I knew I had pushed Jo to work with a boss she hated but then she had got Fabio. She's telling me now she had given up on work. She's telling me now she and Fabio are still happily married.

'And you?' she asks me. She must be wondering about my face, how I've become one of my odyssey's greatest oddities.

She knows how I made Arnaud suffer. He must have told her his version of events, that all I cared about was beauty, power and money. He must have told her of the brawls between him and my powerful boss, then pre-husband, later to become post-husband who can't stand up from his bed and wears a stained gown. He has swapped his whip for a leash, which is there for irony (not sure the whip ever was...). Jo could have ended up working for him! 'I have studied with some of the world's foremost Pilates masters,' I tell her.

'But you were such a banker?' she protests. She can't hold her astonishment.

'¡Quién te ha visto y quién te ve!' I quote a grandmother's favourite saying: who has seen you and who sees you now! 'Different phases,' I say to her, 'different faces,' pointing at my beautiful new face.

It's always only a matter of time for the curtain of the sanctuary to reap, I can sense Jo thinking with her clever little mind, *for clever, well-educated girls to retire to marry their rich colleagues.*

'I received a degree from Patrick K, who studied with Joseph,' I explain. She should know who Joseph is. 'And with Master Raoul.'

Jo looks lost, though, holding to her plastic cup.

I grab a card for her, from a pocket hidden in my tights: Studio EspeCarma. 'My real baby is facial complexion,' I finish in triumph.

'How's your husband?' she asks. Bitch.

My husband had looked an Indian prince to me: beautiful and powerful. I had been so proud of him, paraded him around friends and acquaintances like a catch in the early years of our marriage. But nobody can know where he is now. Nobody other than me, Putri and the Harley doctors.

When I first met Arnaud, who had joined the bank in the same intake as Jo, Fabio and myself, I dismissed him immediately for being shorter than me as well as bald. Months later he had proven to be viciously intelligent and had come to work in Media too. It had been his passion from the start, he had claimed. And that with all the mergers in the space he would keep busy, learn lots. He never admitted to be in it for the money, always maintaining that knowledge went further than cash. He was the intellectual type and his family was well-off anyway.

Arnaud was the first to question my own motivations to join Media, almost from the start. It was a hotspot yes, but he had smelled the competition between me and Jo. How could I get satisfaction solely from keeping someone from what they yearned for? Arnaud pretended to have a noble heart, no thirst for power. No joy in exerting power. He wanted to prod me. He assured me it was because he cared. What exactly was I looking for other than to piss off Jo? He wanted to know.

He never had the courage to face it though.

He knew from the beginning our boss was what I had wanted. To share his power, to grow alongside the man who back then lit my fire. All I have done I did it for my prince.

'My husband is very supportive of my studio,' I tell Jo, which is the truth. Then I look intensely at her face.

She feels analysed and takes her hands to her skin. I see that reaction in my clients all the time.

'*Kokido* means the control of beauty,' I start explaining after a sip of my drink, 'and is somewhat different from any other system of facial massage, more like a manipulation technique.'

Jo nods before I continue but I can tell she's uneasy, perhaps even scared as if in front of a witch.

'It works specifically and precisely with the facial meridians and acupressure points to achieve a balance,' I add. I can imagine she's considering the profound changes my face has been through.

It was only after the birth of my third child that I hung up my work bags and disappeared from view, to another clinic, still in Harley. A nurse in a tiny lift took me to a floor which had no calling button.

In there, I did not exist.

In there, the drugs came in and the hair came out.

My prince nursed me. He nursed me and he cried as he massaged the skin of my bald head. He didn't look powerful anymore. He said he was worried he would lose me. I was more worried of what my body was becoming. If he did not lose me he would leave me. He couldn't do anything about it. Those days tainted everything, their violence breaking us beyond repair. I started to despise him. How could he touch me? How could he caress me? He could not have been physically attracted to me!

That was when I started to think back to Arnaud and the nights we had spent together. Because Arnaud had nothing to do with what was happening to me, and I could imagine that perhaps with him it would have never happened. I could imagine a different life in a parallel universe, as my shell of a husband held me in his trembling hands in that hidden room. I may as well have lived on the moon, a moon where Arnaud and I appeared so united, by a mutual hatred of my prince. In my thoughts Arnaud grunted, 'You should not have married him because such marriages never end in ways which are easy.' In my thoughts Arnaud brought his fingers to my lips and they tasted like the ocean.

Putri is the only one who knows about the Harley room, the one then and the one now. She was there when I came back home, recovered from the cancer. Only, I was not recovered at all. She is the one who helped me when my husband went back to work and the kids to school, because I was surrounded by family and friends but had never been so alone. Putri observed my anxiety, dealt with my panic attacks. What was my biggest fear that was suddenly preventing me to go on living? 'Losing control of my body again.' I became obsessed with it to the point of filling my days with constant body routines and diets, mineral concoctions, fantasies of top-grade frownies, chemical peels, large filler injections, wraps, face savers, VTOX, restylane, microdermabrasion, latis, caci, lightstim... Everyone saw through my post-cancer phase as a natural rebound from a temporary state of disrepair but Putri understood the change had been permanent, a new force coming out from a life-changing experience. She had herself gone through something similar, after escaping her husband who beat her, and she was thankful I had given her a safe home. Within months Putri was encouraging me to read the masters, then meet them to study with them. Nothing would ever again retard my self-actualisation.

 My husband and children were delighted their frail mother had found something to reinvigorate her and occupy her. I would soon start a new life in charge of my own body, gain a new face to live again.

 I turn to Jo.

'We all go to the gym to work out our bodies very early on in life.'

She looks at me as if she didn't.

'We want our body to be toned and healthy,' I add. 'The face and neck, which has ten per cent of our body's muscles should also be exercised to look healthier, with more glow. We can prevent ageing. Trust me,' I smile. 'Studio EspeCarma has an effective routine and you can start at any age.'

Jo looks terrified, as if I had mouthed things, hectoring and incomprehensible. I insist that she check out my videos. She must surely be able to afford at least that if she's still married to Fabio. I have heard he's doing well.

'Look at me!' I force her to look at me but she almost doesn't want to. 'My young cameramen tell me they have hardly seen a fifty-year-old looking like me,' I laugh.

We competed for everything to the guts, me and Jo, and I always felt I had won.

'Look at me! Look at my face!'

I don't want her to feel the slightest hint of pity.

I know Jo can't believe how I got this face. And she's right to think there is more sacrifice behind it than what I am making out. Of course there was.

There was a cell. But at least it was set amongst greenery. There were the monks. There was a woman who brought me leaves and lotus tea and another shaved woman who constantly toyed with my head, for days and days. For days and days my mind had nothing and I felt like someone was changing my blood. And after some weeks my face had changed.

When my prince saw me he moved out.

When he sees me now he doesn't recognise me and talks instead of a woman who could not respond to human touch, a man who threw a key into a fire to cure her fever and saw bubbles of skin rise from the depths. He always ends up asking me to show him the berries.

'I don't recognise you,' Jo is saying. 'But you look great. I will definitely give it a go. I will call you for an appointment one day.'

She will not, she's only looking for an excuse to leave quickly. And when she walks away I down my coffee and briskly return to my oasis, where I feel queen of infinite time and space, hoping for noon appointments.

But a question lingers in my mind: where would I be had I chosen Arnaud?

It was only after the birth of my third child that I hung up my work bags and disappeared from view, to another clinic, still in Harley. A nurse in a tiny lift took me to a floor which had no calling button.

In there, I did not exist.

In there, the drugs came in and the hair came out.

My prince nursed me. He nursed me and he cried as he massaged the skin of my bald head. He didn't look powerful anymore. He said he was worried he would lose me. I was more worried of what my body was becoming. If he did not lose me he would leave me. He couldn't do anything about it. Those days tainted everything, their violence breaking us beyond repair. I started to despise him. How could he touch me? How could he caress me? He could not have been physically attracted to me!

That was when I started to think back to Arnaud and the nights we had spent together. Because Arnaud had nothing to do with what was happening to me, and I could imagine that perhaps with him it would have never happened. I could imagine a different life in a parallel universe, as my shell of a husband held me in his trembling hands in that hidden room. I may as well have lived on the moon, a moon where Arnaud and I appeared so united, by a mutual hatred of my prince. In my thoughts Arnaud grunted, 'You should not have married him because such marriages never end in ways which are easy.' In my thoughts Arnaud brought his fingers to my lips and they tasted like the ocean.

Putri is the only one who knows about the Harley room, the one then and the one now. She was there when I came back home, recovered from the cancer. Only, I was not recovered at all. She is the one who helped me when my husband went back to work and the kids to school, because I was surrounded by family and friends but had never been so alone. Putri observed my anxiety, dealt with my panic attacks. What was my biggest fear that was suddenly preventing me to go on living? 'Losing control of my body again.' I became obsessed with it to the point of filling my days with constant body routines and diets, mineral concoctions, fantasies of top-grade frownies, chemical peels, large filler injections, wraps, face savers, VTOX, restylane, microdermabrasion, latis, caci, lightstim... Everyone saw through my post-cancer phase as a natural rebound from a temporary state of disrepair but Putri understood the change had been permanent, a new force coming out from a life-changing experience. She had herself gone through something similar, after escaping her husband who beat her, and she was thankful I had given her a safe home. Within months Putri was encouraging me to read the masters, then meet them to study with them. Nothing would ever again retard my self-actualisation.

My husband and children were delighted their frail mother had found something to reinvigorate her and occupy her. I would soon start a new life in charge of my own body, gain a new face to live again.

I turn to Jo.

10

Julieta

The front door to the building has been painted red overnight in an act of defiance. Fair Mary stands under the columned portico, her pink trainers slightly apart, her hands on her hips as she faces the door. Her long, dyed ponytail dangles side to side down the back of her thin sapphire sweater. From behind, she looks teenagery in her dark elasticated jeans, colourful citations rainbowed across her legs, even if she celebrated her sixtieth birthday only three days ago. Outside it's snowing.

'Plants and a possible corpse,' she reads from the red door, the letter stuck to it with Blu Tack. She reads almost solemnly, her diction evidencing a posh education she has kept hidden from the rest.

Raoul, tall and slim as a javelin behind her, a man who looks kept on rabbit lettuce and assorted tubers, notices one of the floor tiles is cracked, perhaps from his latest pressure clean; he will call Tom later, the building manager, to have it replaced. He's wearing his own fleece by now and put on a pair of shorts and espadrilles from two summers ago, perfectly inappropriate for the snow. In his shaved musician's head full of hopeful tunes, he's still irresolute about the news and definitely doesn't want to appear too guilty. At least, he wasn't the one who found the corpse.

'She always mad!' Javier acts shocked and uses his mop to steady himself next to Raoul. He was the unfortunate soul to uncover the death scene when attending to Bode's basement flat earlier in the morning. He has told all of them repeatedly how she looked a furred, inert puppet, slumped on her chaise longue, a worn-out book by her hand, her mouth replete with traditional English trifle, though he had not realised what the ball of vomit was at the time.

'Her dog howl and howl!' Javier mock-weeps. 'She good woman!' He likes to claim iron strength. *'Yo vengo de la calle,* I come from the streets,' he often tells the others, but they all know he never sold drugs, he never told lies and he never stole from anybody despite growing up in Mexico City; he is clearly a weakling.

Bode, named after the rebellious queen no doubt, enjoyed irking everybody, and Raoul is convinced this red door, this silly letter, is all part of an elaborate old woman's ruse to pay them back. He curses Mary's childish excitement in digging through it, searching for what exactly? He despises Mary for stepping into the irritating do-gooder territory of justice at any cost.

'You think madame she typed the letter? She paint the door?' Javier's right hand holds a pale blue handkerchief. He blows his nose loudly before he scrunches it into a ball and puts it back into the right pocket of his chestnut trousers.

Mary looks at him in disgust and counts three stains by his groin.

He notices her look and shrugs his tortured muscles. *Me importa un culo,* he's thinking about the stains. He doesn't give a damn.

'Who else!' Raoul knows he should try to sound less exasperated when, suddenly, the building door opens inwards, a large wave of flesh rushing out to collide against Mary's face as she steps back onto Raoul's feet. He screams.

It's Chuck, as big and square as a refrigerator, with his wispy shower hair almost immediately freezing in contact with the cold air. They all know he loves birds, mainly the female kind, psychedelic drugs, indiscretion and to mock people. Even if he would rather stand for wit, virulence and *jouissance* and he claims his dictate in life is 'Live in a funny heart'. This morning he's dangling a blue tie undone over his thick neck, like a snake, as the building door closes behind him.

'What's going on?' he asks chummily, only slightly surprised to see so many neighbours in the small portico at this time of the morning. 'I heard sirens?' he suddenly admits and his eyes fix beyond Raoul and Mary, onto the ambulance by the side of the road directly outside the building gates; its warning had sounded syncopated, he recalls, as if tiresome toddlers (he abhors toddlers) had been playing with buttons.

'It's Bode,' Raoul comes out from behind Mary. 'We had to call an ambulance this morning.' He has a hand to his forehead as if to hold his head. His mind is automatically running a tune appropriate for a funeral.

'The dog howl and howl,' Javier sobs softly again.

Mary mechanically takes her reading glasses up like a visor. They are thin and a flowery yellow. Chuck looks at her face and quickly concludes she's seriously becoming an old hag, her cheeks cut with ravines. It will be bingo wings next if she doesn't get some serious exercise. *All that harsh life in the camps cannot be helping her,* he thinks. 'Did she fall and break her hip?' he asks about Bode, sounding almost cheerful. His body is still blocking the entrance door.

Mary, Raoul and Javier stare at their feet. Raoul finds another broken tile three down from the one he had identified some minutes before. It's a mess.

'She dead, she dead,' Javier whines and is in need of his hanky again.

'Oh,' Chuck doesn't know what to say, fails to come in with an appropriate joke. What a useless head he has this morning!

'It seems she left a message stuck to the door,' Mary tells him as she's trying to get him to shift his body away from the door.

Raoul doesn't want Chuck or anybody else to believe in a message from Bode's grave. What does the bloody letter say? He wishes he had seen it when he came down rushing after Javier, before calling the ambulance this morning.

'Where are the ambulance men?' Chuck's huge mass continues to block the door and Raoul notices he is wearing mismatched socks, one blue and one red.

'Only one. He is downstairs with her.' Mary has now crossed her arms and rests them on her bulging stomach. She's annoyed at Chuck's intrusion and wants to get back to reading Bode's message on the front door. But Chuck won't move.

'Did they not want a next of kin with them?' Chuck passes both his hands along the sides of his shiny jacket, ironing it purposefully or perhaps checking for something in a pocket.

Mary, Raoul and Javier look at their feet again. *Next of kin?* thinks Raoul. *What is Chuck talking about? He knows every soul hated that woman.*

'What's that ambulance doing here?' Someone has just come in from the street across the gates.

It's pretty Olivia, Flat 6's cheeky cherubim. Her bosom bolts forward, under Chuck's close scrutiny. 'Why is our front door red?' Her voice sounds like a squeaky clarinet. She has strolled back from the nearby primary school with Maria from Flat 10. They often enjoy drop-off together with their girls. She had not noticed the door being red when she came out earlier in the morning.

'It's Bode,' warns Mary, turning back to the women and shouting to no one in particular. She suddenly feels too fidgety, like she needs a proper stretch and can't hold her feelings anymore. Next, Olivia sees Mary's face change abruptly, smearing into a grimace. Mary steps forward towards them and starts weeping on Maria's shoulder. Maria glances over Mary's head and Raoul cannot tell if her face is of concern or disgust. He bets she is happy to have her hands busy, holding some early morning groceries, so that she does not have to hug Mary's flaccid body.

Mary should hold herself together, they are all thinking.

Except Javier, who would happily join the two Marys for a hug but he restrains himself, as David's sepulchral voice is heard chanting down the building stairs approaching the main door.

David opens the door to come out of the building into the portico.

Chuck moves aside for him.

'Has someone died?' David jokes and all heads shift to him. He's spot on as always. It's not for nothing David is Exigent's CEO and can consistently speak with fluency and verve, like a million-word motormouth which makes any shite sound seriously intelligent, and true. All neighbours are now gazing at David as if he himself were an apparition.

He's chirpy this morning out in shorts and a dusty T-shirt for a run in the snow. He has barely slept five hours since he arrived from Australia last night. He rushed home from Heathrow Airport for a fuck jolly with an old girlfriend and only finished her off around 3am, when he put her in a taxi. He's happy to be back after months of absence. Sydney is too hot this time of year.

'Madame Bode is kaput, sir. She's kaput.' Javier talks to David with reverence because he's trying to land a cleaning job with him. He currently cleans Raoul's and Bode's flats, the building's inside staircase and the outside steps from the portico to the basement apartments, but knows David needs much polishing for his come-and-go high-class tenants. He currently has his flat serviced by Javier's cousin, however she's going on maternity leave soon and he hopes to be asked to cover.

All eyes are still on David, holding open the building's door. He knows he doesn't give a damn about Javier's piece of news and thinks that Bode had to die soon anyway. And if anything, this is a positive development for the freehold given the woman was a pain in the ass to handle. Behind him, Heng from Flat 7 has appeared with his poodle dog, and David takes the opportunity to pretend he's being forced to move away from the crowded doorframe.

'Morning traffic jam.' David smiles. 'Terrible news.'

'Sneaky fucker,' whispers Raoul under his breath. He doesn't like David.

David's eyes scan the portico down to the gates to the street and lock on pretty Olivia; he suffers a moment of genital malaise as if he had been caught nude in the shower, then recovers to take decisive paces forward through the crowd. He hates his neighbours, can't stand them. He thinks they are a scourge worse than disabled ex-factory workers on mobility scooters and that their Great British Empire is nothing but a collective fantasy! *Are any of them even British?* He's not cruel just exacting. But the new girl... David means Olivia.

He stares at her.

She looks like a dancer. She's cute, fit and fun. Dressed as quintessential Bond material, she promises pussy galore. *She looks so much my type of chick,* David thinks, the kind who failed miserably to gain financial independence and career, amazingly self-sustained in doing little other than making herself sexy all day. *And a foreigner too,* David can tell just by her looks. Which is perfect, because living overseas changes the rules, makes everything permitted. Olivia's petite, curvy dough devilishly tempts David's body mass, which could drive her to a pulp in no time, despite him being less pumped-up than Chuck, he knows. (David regrets sometimes he never went for rugby or American football or whatever Chuck does. *You have a micro-penis,* he thinks of Chuck to make himself feel better. *You have a micron, sometimes you see it then you don't,* he tells Chuck in his mind.)

'I have a meeting,' David finally yells out loud to whoever is listening, still holding Olivia's stare. And it's one of those moments when he thinks they'll definitely fuck, and how she is probably sure of it too. David knows he will doubtlessly put his finger up her asshole one of these nights, wiggle it rhythmically whilst stroking between her legs in counterpoint, before he hits her pretty face. He's convulsing with anticipated pleasure before disappearing onto the street under the flakes. 'I'll return,' he shouts only to Olivia and she smiles, dissolving like an Alka-Seltzer, her red plaited skort a tad too evident against Maria's conservative grey mid-length caftan next to her.

Olivia feels suddenly frisky, her Pavlovian response to the news of Bode's death, undoubtedly. Her response to middle-aged sex boredom; to a pile of pregnancy piss testers building up in her bathroom shelf. She has tried diversions, making more kids being one of them. She has also tried school friends, restaurant friends, then theatre friends and failed at all of them. She constantly dreams of beer, leather, sweaty pornography and mushroom soup, and does not understand what the soup part of her dream means. She's convinced London has enfolded her like a uterine wall; everything in her marriage is corroding, driving her constant need to hurl herself at strangers, opening her heart to sensuous cultures... *Where does this new neighbour suddenly spring out from?* Olivia knows it's either a lover or she'll kill her husband next time he puts the wrong cup in the dishwasher. *Things I should know but never learnt*, she tells herself: *grabbing handsome guys by the balls before they disappear under the snow.*

Heng, with his socks smelling like they were washed last year, tries to move across the crowded portico himself to take the stairs to Bode's basement flat with his poodle, until he's stopped by a loud chorus. He claims he's due to walk Bode's dog out with his own dog in the park. He's diligent regardless of the weather.

'That dog no good howl and howl now,' Javier says pointing to Bode's dog outside her flat. He runs to Heng and hugs him.

Somehow he feels an affinity to Heng, perhaps because they are both unable to speak English properly. But even Javier needs to disentangle himself from his friend after a couple of seconds in search of fresh air. And it's not only the socks – Heng and soap are known to be on strict terms of passing familiarity.

'Dool led? Dool led!' Heng eventually recovers himself from Javier's affluence of emotion and points to the door thumbs up, offering everyone a toothy smile. Next his poodle wails, shivering from the cold.

They make a jester act, the boy and the dog, having both gobbled too many burritos, foil and all, since they landed in London, dressed in matching vintage school uniforms; Heng's with a note hanging from his pocket from a doctor attesting for his seborrhoeic dermatitis. It's a farce!

And to Raoul's tidy mind, the circus unfolding in front of him is quickly becoming unbearable and he prefers to look away towards the street gates where Olivia rests dreaming, possibly of David's hands, or of dousing her pains with alcohol and chants, Maria still standing like a soldier next to her, probably scheming about Xmas baskets (she's known to be unmatched in that area).

'Madame hurt, she hurt and ambulance with her this morning,' Javier speaks to Heng as if he were a defenceless child and makes signs with his hands, folding them into his heart for hurt and letting them flit around over his head for siren.

Heng draws an 'o' with his mouth and then nods and tries to get back into the building. But Mary is blocking the entrance door.

As Mary moves to let Heng back in, Eva from Flat 3 is coming out, walking languidly like a winter queen carrying an imaginary pile of books over her head, oozing petulance. Her chest is decorated with guns and crucifixes for a mystical touch and she wears a shawl over her shoulders, presumably to keep her bare arms warm.

For Raoul Eva is pure inspiration, her head an empty room with all the windows open. And he loves that weight to her glance as she looks at Bode's sad-looking potted poinsettia twigs by the gates. Heng's knees instead wobble at the sight of her, as he's convinced she drowns babies in their sleep; he steps back to let Eva pass with her silver bike she pulls alongside, her inseparable companion. Chuck freezes; he calls Eva 'ovaries from space' and has dreams of her sleeping with her bike, screwing it, only because she once refused his advances and he likes to think of her as weird, even if deep down he yearns to lay his hand on her clothed knee and share with her his puppy eyes and his spliff, to help orchards in his heart bloom full of craving and desire.

Eva may or may not know of the strength of feelings she evokes amongst her neighbours, but she doesn't greet anybody or ask any questions; about the ambulance, or the fact that there is a crowd hanging around in freezing weather under the building's portico this morning. She simply leads her wheels gracefully down the front steps, squeezing through her neighbours' bodies, to the street. Maria and Olivia move themselves promptly to each side to make space, Maria nearly kneeling in the muck. And when Mary sees the girls curtsying to Eva, even a little, she feels her pancreas on fire, until the femme fatale carries her smell away with her.

Mary, Raoul, Chuck, Maria, Olivia, Javier and Heng are left outside the building in a daze.

It's started to snow more heavily and Raoul is the first to come out of his stupor to urge Olivia and Maria to join the rest of them under the portico before they look like Christmas trees.

Mary has closed the door to the building and puts her reading glasses back down to take to the letter on the door once more, glowing against the fresh red paint. 'The Plants. Some of the comments:' she excels at making punctuation come alive.

'Which plants?' Olivia asks over Mary's shoulder and Raoul looks sheepish.

'"I'm happy for the plants to remain. I like a bit of greenery,"' Mary has read in a feminine voice as if she were impersonating perhaps Olivia.

'That's me,' says Maria, who has moved by Olivia's side. I told her that. Maria looks at the plants lining the walls on the inside of the gates, the ones Eva stared at on her way out. They look brown. But they did look green with occasional pink flowers last spring.

'"… I would like the plants to stay,"' Mary reads again from the letter, trying to sound like a man this time. 'Chuck, is that your comment?' she asks.

'I don't remember. Perhaps my girlfriend wrote it.' His voice is baritone, naturally.

'I thought Bode and your girlfriend hated each other's guts, that they never talked to each other.'

Chuck shrugs annoyed. 'Emily always behaves wonderfully to old people.' He suddenly wishes he had claimed a busy schedule at work and left immediately this morning, like David.

"'Personally I love your plants and I am very happy with them,'" Mary reads on. 'Is that you, Olivia?'

'I didn't write back.' Olivia offers a poker face from behind Mary.

'Why?' Mary is clearly imagining herself at one of her refugee camps, expected to be straight and forceful with her subjects because she knows otherwise situations like this turn to revolution.

'I've been busy with a tap-dancing competition coming up, and,' she's hesitant, 'I have a lot on with my daughter at a new school...' The reality is the invitation to comment on Bode's plants agitated Olivia and she declined to comment.

Olivia's excuses make Chuck sigh. Olivia the victim annoys him. He had her home for a drink last month, courtesy of his girlfriend Emily, who claimed they should help themselves amongst Americans, and his neighbour played the victim from the moment she sat on his couch. She told them how she married at sixteen to a jerk and was pregnant by her last year of school. That she only managed to run away from him when he joined a demonic sect, after tricking a British BBC crew into helping her, then marrying her as soon as her divorce came through. Chuck, who had been so excited ahead of Olivia's visit, yawned throughout. It was like Olivia thought the world owed her for her troubles. And he could see it in their faces, Heng's, Javier's, even Raoul's, how men all over the world fell for pretty Olivia (like he once had). Even David... It made him sick.

'Anyway, why should I explain myself to you? Did you answer to Bode's plant plea yourself?' Olivia shows her teeth to Mary and Maria puts her hands up calling for peace.

'I wasn't here.' Mary looks intently at Olivia's pretty face. 'Some of us have more important things to do than tap competitions, you know!' She spells it out to Olivia, in her best school head-teacher tone, how she thinks most women nowadays so unsubstantial. Mary sometimes wishes she was not alone saving the world! Still she has to say it how it is, to keep firm. She puts her hands to her hips again and turns back to the page stuck to the red door, 'Raoul: "I hate the plants,"' she intones in a deathly rattle.

Mary, Raoul, Chuck, Maria, Olivia, Javier and Heng all look at their shoes, again. A baby snail is leaving a trail as it strolls right past Raoul's left espadrille, from one of Bode's plant pots. He crushes it.

Suddenly, an ambulance man is coming up Bode's steps from the basement, commanding everyone's attention.

'She totally dead, madame?' Javier sniffs to the man as he reaches for his pocket.

'The police will arrive shortly,' the man answers, talking to all of them.

Raoul thinks he's winking.

'We can't move the corpse,' he explains further 'but morgue services will do so after the police agree to it and you should all remain available for now.' Then the man moves towards the ambulance to grab a banana.

'What a fucking charade!' Raoul curses loud enough for all to hear.

Chuck really wishes he had rushed to work.

Olivia bubbles with childhood excitement for what this new adventure may bring, and Maria knows, as a Christian, she should feel more sorry than she does about the whole affair.

'Whal's loing on?' Heng asks the ambulance man, as he's back peeling his post-death banana. He needs a repeat of his instructions.

'Can someone take care of the woman's dog?' the driver asks looking at Bode's dog, unusually silent, tied outside the dead woman's flat. 'You?' he holds Heng's stare.

Heng nods, still lost.

'Has anyone told Carla!' Mary has remembered out of the blue. They all know Carla in Flat 8 is the only neighbour who befriended Bode.

'I will knock on her door,' offers Maria. And as she's pushing open the door to the building, to run upstairs for Carla, she sees it at the bottom of Bode's letter, the signature: 'Julieta.' Bode's pen name is Julieta.

An hour before…

'Mr Raoul open, *abra! Abra! Hay un muerto!*'

Raoul's Spanish is rudimentary at best from his last spiritual healing trip to some ruins in Peru. And Javier is always so melodramatic about one thing or another; his body hunched over the hoover often turns Raoul on, but he could never put up for long with such an edgy partner plus all the facial hair would drive him mad (even if Javier shaves at least once a week, according to him).

Raoul finally opens the door to his flat.

Javier does not even flinch at the flamingo-print boxy Armani briefs in front of him, which Raoul bought in Singapore when he was last with Sir John's crowd on an 'errand'. Had Javier been in a fit state, he would have thought Raoul's 'shorts' way too tight, though nothing as forward as his nude six-pack glistening only inches from Javier's own nose. But in his current haze, the cleaner simply grabs Raoul by the arm, dragging him out, coconut and ginger juice overflowing from Raoul's cup on his hand all the way down the staircase. They leave the door to Raoul's flat open and Raoul protests he has not even had time to grab a vest top.

Raoul is scared as he bends his head down to enter Bode's flat in the basement; her dog is barking outside her door, tied to the entrance staircase. He feels as if he were trespassing through a towering oak arch warning him from entering Bode's cultural arcana (as she once called it), sneaking in via a tiny portal hinged within he knows he was never supposed to cross.

Inside, it's wasteland dark and it smells epistolary. Or perhaps it's only damp floorboards under the damp carpeting; the odour of cathedrals and encyclopedias: it feels sepulchral to Raoul. He's entering the underworld, becoming a little more black and a little more dead with every step. From the corridor he can see straight into the living room, Bode's famous chaise longue on which Raoul distinguishes an inert body shape. Raoul and Javier approach the body.

'It is a dead, not moving. *Un muerto*,' Javier explains.

Raoul makes a sign to Javier that he can stop talking, that he has got the gist of things. He realises only then that his feet are nude and cold and he scratches his toes against Bode's carpet, disgusted. He looks for somewhere to rest his coconut juice and decides on Bode's desk by the chaise. 'Call an ambulance now,' he orders Javier, who is theatrically tippy toeing behind him.

Javier's eyes scan efficiently through Bode's desk's surface like the good thief of little things that he is, until they land on a yellow piece of paper: 'Call this AMBULANCE,' followed by a number. *Madame must have left note in case she died, her personal ambulance,* Javier thinks. *Madame highly preoccupied 'bout dying and lived prepared.* Javier takes the yellow paper and walks outside into the morning snow, his mobile in hand.

Raoul sighs a lonely sigh. Then he gets to work like a clever investigator checking the crime scene.

Bode's barrel-like body splattered on the chaise wears an old bison and a ciggie holder; *making her look something that she never was,* thinks Raoul. The fur advances an entirely false impression of the woman as a slap my butt and you will eat the copy machine kind of kinky self-assured girl who kicked ass. *Why she never gave a damn to age appropriately!* Raoul breathes deep.

Bode's thick, sagging lips are smeared in glossy lipstick, or is it a kind of food or vomit, clashing with the thin orange mop slanted over her forehead. Raoul imagines her swallowing Nembutal, handful after handful, and lying down on her chaise waiting for death as streams of poison entered her blood. *Is she nude under the coat, a gold-plated revolver fastened to an emerald silk garter?* Raoul gags. *So theatrical.* He disapproves more than approves, really, despite being an artist himself. Perhaps Bode dreamed herself in a gothic alcove arranged inside a courtyard, the chaise longue on cold paving stones, books on her breasts, her obeying lover making her his mistress, feeding her trifle, a mistress of a castle, a leading sultana ancient and profound who would never be trivial. 'Never met a girl like you before!' Raoul tells the corpse as he de-coats his old neighbour, high on adrenaline...

But she is wearing a robe underneath.

'*La robe*,' it comes to Raoul in French, a funky cloth, like a comforter more than a fashionable garment. French makes him sound sophisticated. Underneath the lumpy body, the sheet covering the chaise is black silk, monogrammed, and Raoul almost saddens at his neighbour's final efforts to look amatory. *Yet she never mingled with anyone other than to drive them to despair...* he thinks. Did Raoul really know her? Is he pigeonholing her? 'Good times cannot last forever,' he tells the corpse sniggering, and covers the robe again with the coat before turning to the surrounding the decor.

Books, books and books on shelves.

Otherwise, a spring of plastic oranges hangs from a rack, meaning to be ornamental. There's plenty of other tacky gift items around too, probably manufactured in Taipei; Raoul checks their backs for confirmation of his suspicions and is proud his flair had put him close. A lonely picture on another ledge: four old-looking, ugly men posing with the background of the Cotopaxi, a faraway volcano he recognizes from another therapeutic trip. *Is one of them Bode's dead husband?*

'Wooden shagging doll, clonk, clonk,' suddenly the words come to Raoul's mouth, out of hidden corners of his crazy mind.

He's thinking what Bode's husband would say if he saw her

now. 'I may have married a pretentious ugly peasant but I used to fuck good whores, stub out my fags in pretty cunts.' He had worked in the docks in Cape Town. He was proud of it. Was she proud of him? Had his bad manners turned her on? Now she looked as doomed as she had ever looked alongside her husband, and never in a romantic way.

Raoul stares closely at Bode's face. Her eyelashes heavy like frog fingers, definitely too much make-up. *Could the lip gloss vomit really be trifle?* A strange torsion of her muscles spells a superhuman effort. 'We live in Dickens,' he has heard that said somewhere and repeats it to the corpse.

Perhaps Bode was trying to be a literary character. Certainty she had her vanity, of writing well. She claimed her words cut like a razor. She was a witch of the pen although they all just called her a bookish weirdo. 'In between wallpapering my lounge and bathroom I wrote The Paper Creep,' she had once told them. They had never read it. She didn't come across as a good writer anyway, the word fuck or one of its variants prominent in her every line of email rant to them, perhaps a habit in an effort to be understood by her husband. She used to pontificate obscenities aloud too whilst planting. She was a rude trumpet, a machine gun of unwelcome consciousness in the language of her husband the docker, a puke of psychosis from which there could be no relief.

'You were definitely a wild ride,' Raoul says, searching inside Bode's eyes. 'What glorious self-immolation. A howl against death. Is this final *mis en scène* supposed to be a *classico*, Bode?' Raoul likes his Italian (as well as his French) when he can remember it. This whole set-up defies his logic but it kind of arouses him too. 'I'm glad how I've come to be in your room with you,' he says, smiling at Bode's dead lump. He had never let her in his house before and neither had she, even if she had drawn him, like everyone else, closer and closer, through hate; but never too close.

Raoul leaves the chaise to inspect Bode's desk and only then realises an elaborate table for one has been set on it. 'You really emptied the whole bloody cutlery, Bode!' he roars. 'And all just for trifle?'

The next thing Raoul sees is Bode's computer on a far corner of the desk. It dates back at least fifty years and he is almost surprised the screen background isn't green. It's showing a magnified picture of Bode's outside petunias, or whatever plants they are; the ones Raoul hates. There's considerable text underneath the on-screen picture, which Raoul reads.

'I would like to thank everyone who wrote to me to say how much they have enjoyed the plants over the years. I should have twigged when Raoul venomously spat between his clenched teeth that he "hated" the plants and that he was going to get fucking rid of them.'

Raoul swallows nervously and tries to steady himself then continues reading.

'He has repeatedly damaged the plants, claiming to punish them for being a fucking "fire" hazard and a "trip" hazard (in thirty-seven years not one person has bloody tripped), and for "devaluing" the building. Some of the agapanthus,' *so that's what they are*, Raoul thinks almost cheerfully, 'come from the national living collection.' 'Bollocks,' he denies Bode's truths, 'they surely don't.' 'He also hates dogs and children,' Raoul continues reading, 'and will surely be happy to know he's driving me to my fricking death.'

Raoul has read enough.

He doesn't hate dogs and children particularly. He is about to close this death letter of sorts and delete it immediately. But a compulsion comes from deep inside him to read on after all...

'When decking was built in the building, lots of timber left over was fucking dumped in the flowerbed despite being more than thirty-five years old, and to throw away a natural resource casually has given us a depleted ozone layer.' Raoul is relieved this sentence alone is enough proof that whatever Bode writes or wrote is dribble nobody should give credit to. 'I saved the decking and wanted to build flower boxes but unfortunately I was paralysed unexpectedly, fucking shit, and now the timber too has to go? Obsessive compulsives like Raoul—' *I'm not that at all!* he's vexed again, '—are cunts who latch onto things and whilst the house may be burning down, they are fucking preoccupied with fixing a dripping tap. He will be the death of us all one day, fucking hell!'

Raoul feels indignant and stops for a deep breath.

'Once again thank for your support, compliments and kindness,' he glances at the end of Bode's letter plunged into a momentary murderous trance. He shuts the file down and presses delete. 'Fuck that,' he whispers under his breath into his own nude torso, 'this bitch's heart attack has nothing to do with me.'

It's cold in Bode's flat but Raoul's body is burning.

Morality out of raw emotion. Instinctive feelings are good. Heart without brain. History speaking with the voice of the endless crowd, of neighbours who hated Bode; Raoul feels one of history's elect with a well-curated toilet-brush moustache, even if history has taught us that men with mustaches should never be handed positions of power. He almost has an urge to pee on Bode's carpet, right next to her dead body by the chaise, in an act of pure defiance. Then remembers he does not have his shoes on.

A window with Bode's inbox has popped up from behind the file Raoul has sent to the trash: he has a discovery moment: he searches for emails from David from Flat 10, and studies the results for a few minutes.

The expletives Raoul comes across are worse than he thought, worse than Bode's; *David is a pro!*

He takes his time on a curious, unexpected find, a message from Chuck with David cc'ed, where Chuck threatens he will use David's law firm to sue Bode if she continues to be mean to his girlfriend Emily. *Interesting...*

Raoul has never liked Chuck's girlfriend himself and thinks Chuck could do so much better, especially if he jumped to the other side. But he concludes the written word in the message is not compelling enough in this case, not what he is looking for exactly.

There is another email that grabs his attention though, with Bode giving instructions to Maria, with all tenants cc'ed, regarding her possible death. Maria obviously ignored it as there's no reply in the thread. Raoul doesn't recall having ever received this email himself: 'This week some fucking outrage happened in Kensington High Street and as a result I thought I ought to say something,' he reads Bode's lines. 'An old woman fell and had either a heart attack or a stroke and she was lying on the pavement. I had a stroke in May 2011; I was paralysed down my right side and suffered permanent neural damage.' Raoul scowls at Bode's eternal incoherence and self-preoccupation. 'My balance has been affected and if I fall backwards I cannot get up off the floor,' he reads on. 'I have fallen twice in my fucking garden on a workday morning and there was no one in House 13a or House 13c. Either I found a way back onto my feet on my own or I would have had to fucking lie on the ground for maybe seven hours until someone came home. Eventually, I managed to worm my legs into a hole and with a great effort got back onto my feet,' he's growing impatient at Bode's long-windedness. 'This will probably happen again, so if you find me flat on my back cursing loudly, then probably all I will need is some help getting back onto my feet. If I am flat on my back and silent please leave me and call an ambulance. If I am not breathing please call for an ambulance and the police,' Raoul starts laughing outright at his neighbour's madness. 'I have dealt with two deaths of our neighbours. One was fucking notorious and had me bashing a constable over the head to make the stupid man realise that he was manhandling a fucking eighty-year-old woman for murder when her husband had died of cancer!' He takes a sip of his coconut juice next to him to give him strength. 'Now, as I will probably only have a ten-minute warning, you may have to deal with my body, Maria.' 'Lucky you!' Raoul cheers in a whisper. 'If Flora is about—' Bode's referring to Maria's pest of a child even if Raoul insists to himself he doesn't hate all children '—please attend to her first.'

Raoul wonders where on earth Javier has gone.

Next his mind drifts back to the strange fixation Bode always had with Flora, Maria's child, and the baskets of books that used to clutter Flat 11's pigeon hole until the day they suddenly stopped, not that long ago. He always hated Flora for racing up and down the stairs for them. Or perhaps he resented more her mother Maria, whose extremely logical arguments at tenant meetings drove him crazy, until Raoul pleaded to her husband to attend alone; 'Her husband can at least accept the flaws of logic, that there is no valid reasoning when fighting crazy neighbours,' he had come clean with Chuck about Maria. 'Maria might as well focus exclusively on raising her beloved child, making her into another loopy brainchild like her, and leave all else to her husband,' Chuck had agreed. 'Has she not always been overprotective of that child?'

Raoul thinks; he enjoys plotting in search of an alternative guilty party for Bode's death. Did Bode's love for Flora get to Maria, who confronted her?

'Effectively I have a fucking time bomb in my head,' Bode's message to Maria goes on delivered by Raoul's voice. 'I can only stay on my feet for four hours at a time. Re-potting and re-planting is a bit of a stop-and-start event so it will take me a bit of time.' *She's talking her poinsettias again!* he curses. 'My next birthday is my sixty-fifth—' *No bloody way!* he doesn't buy that '—but the doctors think I may not make it—' *That's right,* he nods '—so it may be the last year of the plants—' *Those bloody plants again* '—and I.' 'Hallelujah,' Raoul expresses gratitude for an instant. 'When and where I will pop my clogs is anybody's guess.' *Not anymore,* he smiles. 'I apologise, Maria, if you are fucking stuck with my sudden death. Please let me thank you in advance. Once again thank you for your support, compliments and kindness.'

Raoul let's out a deep, deep groan.

He can tell there's something unsavoury between Bode and Maria, between Bode and Chuck, but there's not enough to establish irrevocable culpability. And Javier is not back yet. So he scrolls down the inbox further, at greater speed, under pressure to find a more incriminatory piece of evidence against whoever, preferably against David.

'Last week I was going backwards and forwards to hospital and David was sitting in his window watching my comings and goings,' Raoul has stopped on an older email to all tenants. 'He insists on a fucking sterile, lavatorial, dead area as our entrance yet is building a frickin' hideous golden mausoleum high above our heads, which can be seen from miles beyond the park.' *She's dead right,* Raoul nods. He complained of it himself. 'Does nobody care about all the regulations he's fucking infringing with his sky-high pergola?' he busies himself back to Bode's words. 'The communal vote to keep our roof a roof is irrelevant to him. I have inflicted a restraining order on my and my dog's behalf, not to come close to the fucking vicious man, to protect us. Because a heart attack will be fatal next time.' Raoul stirs with excitement for words so perfect. 'Twice last week I was wearing a heart monitor and David defied me, my heartbeat raising so fast that the monitor could not fucking record it. The monitor cut out after David's total dismissal of the roof vote and I wanted you all to know in case you find me dead one day.'

Raoul claps wholeheartedly.

'Once again thank for your support, compliments and kindness,' he finishes reading the email. Next he maximises the message to fit the full computer screen and finally finds himself at peace.

As he's about to leave in search of Javier, who is taking an inexplicable amount of time, *perhaps simply because he's a halfwit*, thinks Raoul, he suddenly spots a cheque to him. To Javier the cleaner. On the desk by his juice.

Raoul is surprised the sod hasn't taken it with him this morning.

He reads the words, 'Javier, final cheque,' on a sticky note on top. Why final? Had Javier not been doing his job properly? Raoul is surprised. He knows there had been previous cleaners, dozens. Some stole or were suspected of it, some had an inappropriately good figure which made Bode feel bad about herself, she claimed. Raoul himself does not have any complains about Javier's cleaning, would happily offer the poor man some extra hours. Other than for the CDs that went missing once, nothing has been amiss for months. Perhaps Javier has stolen some of Bode's precious books? 'You would be doing us a favour, mate!' he exclaims aloud, surrounded as he is by thousands of editions the freehold's management has for years been blaming for the subsidence of the building.

Still, Raoul was not the one opposed to paying for Bode's subsidence troubles… Adam from Flat 5 was – another potential culpable for her death? Adam was the only one to deny her, with his financial mastermind that has led him to sell everything his wife once owned and move out to the countryside, where he now lives rearing goats, still calling himself a top-notch Notting Hill-based property manager when he only has a one-bedroom flat which he puts up on Airbnb.

Where does Bode get all these books from anyway? Rubbish skips. Dead friends. Closing libraries, thinks Raoul. 'The trash in this flat...' he curses scanning around himself, completely nude but for his briefs. 'And she probably thinks they are worth something.' He remembers Bode boasting more than once that she made a six-figure salary selling second-hand books. He can't help sniggering.

'Javier!' Raoul calls having rushed to the apartment's front door but there's no answer.

Coming back to Bode's living room to retreat from the cold, he suddenly makes something by Javier's cheque: a medical certificate. No, a blood test result. The blood test is from a vet though. It must be for Bode's dog although it says a poodle. *It must be for Heng's dog.* 'SHIT!' It has rabies. 'It should be put down,' Raoul speaks in horror. Infections make him nervous.

But the test was paid for by Bode. Did Heng know Bode had been investigating his dog?

The fact is Chuck, Maria, David, Javier, Adam, Heng… any of them could have wanted Bode's death. And Raoul's feet are going cold. His chest is going cold too. Should he borrow the cardie he saw hanging from Bode's bathroom door as he came in?

Never in a million years, the infection fear comes up again. 'Javier, Javier, where are you?' he shouts nearing the front door once more, towards the snow outside.

He does take Bode's cardie from her bathroom in the end and promises himself he will shower as soon as he is back in his flat. But as he grabs it, he sees something on the back of Bode's toilet door: a dartboard. It's directly opposite Bode's loo, at the right distance and height. There's something unexpected at its centre...

'Bode, Bode…' Raoul giggles.

It has taken him a bit to realise that it's a face; the board has a picture of a face glued to it. He's scared to his bones it may be his, forcing him to destroy yet more incriminating evidence from the crime scene, even if shredding thrills him, helps him feel as if his actions can count. But the face… the face is female. 'It's Eva's!' he shouts in joyful horror. Even if he's also kind of disappointed. But he's kind of relieved too. Bode didn't only hate him but the whole world, and some people she hated more viciously than him, perhaps.

Underneath the board in nice italic calligraphy Raoul reads, 'You bitch, your cooking smells of decaying faeces.' *Not as bad as Adam's Thai tenants last month,* he reminds himself as he recalls the smell of durian in the staircase.

SOUR PRICKS

Raoul finally hears Javier trodding down the stairs into Bode's flat and runs back to the living room, where he re-takes his coconut drink in his hand and sips on it casually.

'All done!' Javier cheers. 'What a mess in flat eh,' he sighs. 'Should have cut her wrists in garden?'

'Javier!' Raoul shouts like a whining coyote at the cleaner, putting his insensitivity down to shock. Yet he can't get the image out of his brain, of arteries slack like cables. He suddenly feels like Indiana Jones stuck with useless helpers in a dangerous tomb, without a good looking girl. But what use would he make of such a girl anyway?

'To the loo. This emergencies gave me piss,' Javier retorts happily as he runs into Bode's toilet. He has not commented on the flowery jumper covering Raoul's torso, although he has noticed. He has put it down to Raoul being queer.

Raoul busies his hand opening and closing Bode's desk drawer whilst he listens to Javier's thunderbolt of pee. He hopes the repeated movement of his arm can help calm him as well as build his arm muscle.

At an instant when the drawer opens, little torn pieces of eye, ear and nose paper shine at him. Yet another of Bode's enemies? Not Eva again? But when he checks, it's Olivia's daughter, whatever her name is. *She who used to love Bode's dog and play in Bode's overgrown garden together with Maria's child, Flora,* he's quickly putting pieces together. Raoul used to see them from his back window but has not for some time. *It's amazing how things have been degenerating as of late without me taking enough notice,* he thinks as Javier comes out of Bode's toilet.

Next they run up to Raoul's flat for some shoes and a change and back down to wait for the ambulance.

By the front door.

After the ambulance man has finished his banana and given Bode's dog to Heng, and Maria has run to alert Carla upstairs, Raoul invites Mary, Chuck, Olivia, Javier and Heng, with the condition he will come dog-free, to his flat for tea. In Raoul's living room, Chuck compliments Raoul on a vintage guitar hanging on the wall and plays the host with him until everyone is comfortably seated, then accompanies Raoul into the kitchen to make the drinks.

Meanwhile Maria arrives with Carla, who looks numb with shock. She has suspended, in order to come down to her neighbours, a most important project she was working on which she will not disclose. She's is in her usual dress code, trendy perhaps in Yemen. *Age fades her like a blanket,* Maria is busy judging, and thinks Carla is plumper every day despite repeated claims she started a strict diet at age twelve.

Someone who opened Raoul's door to them urgently brings Carla tap water from the kitchen, as if it was a matter of life or death, in a green Harrods mug. She takes it as she's putting her shoes off in the hall to place them alongside everyone else's; Raoul's house is a no-shoes zone. She holds onto the mug tightly and produces a bottled bit of nervous laughter.

Maria proposes to sit her in the living room, in a corner, set her nice, warm and quiet, with a Quality Street she remembers she put in her skirt pocket earlier in the morning, for her daughter. However, when Carla enters the living room and sees Mary, there's no stopping her. Their decades-old rivalry is back.

'I heard Bode shout at you yesterday, over the ivy!' Carla suddenly cries at Mary, and Maria has to restrain her from jumping at Mary's throat, as if loyalty to Bode suddenly rode in Carla's blood alongside witchcraft spells.

Mary retires, whining into a corner of the room.

'She hated your poisonous ivy deeply rooting itself in her garden wall, making it crumble,' Carla yells, hysterical, her Harrods mug shaking in her hand. And everyone is astounded because they have never heard Carla say a loud word before; never a bad word. Not even against Mary who they all know she detests.

Olivia instinctively rushes up from Raoul's sofa to hug Mary in her corner. Chuck pops his head out from the kitchen to see Javier and Heng grinning, their four thumbs up, then he goes back inside and Mary follows him, abandoning Olivia.

'Come on Carla,' says Maria sweetly. 'Bode just had a heart attack like she had been announcing for years.'

Carla's body rocks back and forth in her uniform, until she can be convinced to take a seat on the sofa.

'Ol it could be David's pelgola.' Heng's big mouth.

Maria sends him a funny look.

'Or Dutch witch cooking. Sure was sending madame Bode mad,' Javier's primeval-looking hand taps Heng's bony knee and they both laugh slightly out of sequence, looking like an advert for 111. The jester and the idiot. Maria sends them a double funny look.

Meanwhile in the kitchen, Mary complains to Chuck and Raoul about Carla trying to make her feel guilty. When Raoul shows little compassion, she reminds him, 'What about the red door? With the email about the plants stuck to it? It's a clear suicide note Bode has left stuck to the building's door, with your name on it!'

Raoul jumps back. 'Everyone had their motive!' he protests, smiling gently, then draws Mary and Chuck close to him. 'First,' he announces anticipatorily, 'Javier was about to get sacked by Bode!'

'He kept that quiet!' Mary is less teary all of a sudden. She always saw Javier as scum, the scum she has to deal with day in and day out in her camps. It's just he has made it to her precious England.

'And Heng...' Raoul continues, 'well did you know his poodle has rabies?'

'Is that why you have insisted on having it chained outside in the snow?' Chuck prods. 'How do you know?'

'No way!' Mary is interrupting. 'Bode would have never let her dog close to a rabies dog. Never. She would have had Heng's dog put down!'

'Precisely,' Chuck and Raoul declare in unison. 'Elementary, my dear Watson!' adds Chuck, proud of Raoul's investigative skills, and Raoul beams.

'Anything on Olivia?' Chuck asks, thinking back to the recent time she refused him after having provoked him for days with her short skirts and plunging necklines, her girlie tresses imitating her daughter's. Her husband travels too much but it's still not proper to falsely tempt another man like that.

'Well, she's no innocent cookie either!' it's Raoul's time to shine and Mary and Chuck are all ears. 'Did you know she had pimped her daughter to Bode just to have her on her side, because she felt in need of friends as a newcomer to the building? But Bode must have realised something was odd...'

'What do you mean?' Things don't add up for Mary.

'I found a photograph of the kid shredded to pieces inside a drawer in Bode's desk!'

Chuck and Mary show surprise.

'And I wasn't prying,' Raoul is quick to add.

The three of them glisten with delight as they carry the tea like a virgin in a procession into Raoul's leaving room.

Carla sips her water then hurls again. 'It was you, bitch, what do you say for yourself!' She's looking at Mary once more.

'Bode had a heart attack it's not like she was murdered,' Chuck's deep voice aims to calm the waters. 'And for all we know, many of us had caused her upset.'

'Me innocent,' Javier puts his hands up like in a cowboy movie. Both his hands are free because a real man drinks no tea. Meanwhile Heng is looking in contemplation at the floating flakes through Raoul's terrace doors.

'Bode was about to fire you, Javier.' Chuck smiles fatherly at him. He had himself been about to offer Javier a cleaning contract for his own flat but not anymore. 'And you, my dear Heng, your poodle is ruined and you kept it from her.' Heng remains focused on the terrace doors; perhaps he has not understood Chuck.

'Let's not start name-calling.' Maria's posture changes on the sofa next to Carla. 'We all knew you yourself had threatened to sue the dead woman,' she warns her eyes fixed on Chuck's, 'only because she had asked for your girlfriend to stop smoking on the staircase which, by the way, is *not allowed.*'

Chuck wishes Maria would go back to live in Madrid, *Thank God for Brexit!* He is all for the US–UK special relationship. But for now he is awfully aware her husband is a big fish in the City and they occasionally need to do business together, so he stays quiet.

'Well, we all know you yourself felt threatened by the obsession Bode had for your daughter,' Mary attacks Maria and Maria makes a 'go fuck yourself' face to her.

Two Marys bicker, thinks Raoul as he moves his head from side to side. Mary hates the bankers and especially their wives. So does Maria herself, really. They could get on if only they tried. *What a sorry bunch,* Raoul's brain returns to overdrive. *All so different. Rich and poor. Old and young. Arty and viscerally scientific. Genius and the plain stupid. No wonder we can never understand each other.* He remembers out of the blue, the biggest row of all, when the freehold ended up paying over twenty grand to various lawyers to exchange threatening letters between tenants about which colour to paint the building. It ended plain white; Raoul wishes it had been lilac.

Olivia squeaks but is stopped in her tracks. 'And your daughter was permanently demoted to be nobody under Bode's eyes and you resented that,' rainbow Mary tells her off whilst winking at Raoul.

'Well, what about the fucking note on the bloody front door. What about the fucking plants! Is there an indication of guilt clearer than that?' Olivia looks like a cheap majorette and Raoul hates her more than ever.

'Can we all stop!' Maria has had enough. 'Bode just died of bad health, of old bloody age!' She's so fucking tired of being landed with all this community work. Yes, this is what she calls it, fucking community work. How she wishes she was still toiling in her towering headquarters, which is the only reason she came to this country… but no… it's only her husband being allowed to do that now.

'What 'bout Mr David?'

'What about him, Javier?' Raoul pushes the conversation away from the plants. The pergola is perfect.

'Monster, monstrosity in his terrace upstairs!' Javier is stretching his arms to Raoul's ceiling. 'And then he's run away this morning!'

'He has a point,' Raoul adds fuel to the fire, pensively. As if he had just thought of it.

'And Adam?' says Chuck.

Chuck is always there when you don't want him, Raoul curses inside but smiles at him. Just when everything was going so well and he was about to succeed making David who once dared call him a puff their scapegoat…

'Adam what?' asks Olivia, having recovered from her fierceness and happy to chum with Chuck, a fellow American.

'He was the only one who opposed Bode's work to stop the damp and rot in her flat,' Chuck feels a lion with Olivia on his side, 'claimed it was all her own fault and that she and her book collection should sink to the bottom of the earth where her Julio Verne vintage editions could find a fit end!' He's enjoying the spotlight until he looks at his socks; they are odd, different colours. It blocks him.

'So Bode goes and kills herself as payback?' asks Mary, sounding dubious. 'Or she was so worried about her fate it triggered her stroke? What are you saying? Adam is miles away and the brawl happened months ago if I remember well.' Mary has always liked Adam, but nobody else comes to his defence.

'He is such a jerk,' speaks out Carla. 'Bode was about to vote to stop him putting his flat for rent on that dubious website, sure he was bringing unsavoury characters to our doorstep...'

Nobody is running Carla's expression or posture through their lie detector to tell them how ecstatic she feels behind her grim face, already making plans for a feast following Bode's inheritance.

'Adam or David then?' Raoul pushes his neighbours like clients in a betting shop, as Mary walks out barefoot into his terrace, for air. The tiles are covered in snow.

Heng falls abruptly out of his trance. 'But the nole, the nole to the dol... she painted the dol led, vely led...'

But everybody dismisses Heng, turning instead to a shout from outside. It's Mary, 'It's Bode, it's Bode.' She's screaming at the terrace doors.

All neighbours rush to the snow.

They can see Bode being taken out on a stretcher, Cleopatra-style, under the flakes. She's waving gracefully. The ambulance driver has untied her dog who is jumping onto her lap. Bode is mouthing to them all, 'Love you,' and blowing them kisses, alongside the ever-winking ambulance man.

'Madame is life,' Javier screams. 'No possible.'

'Lulieta, lulieta!' cries Heng but nobody understands what he is on about.

'What's this fucking joke?' Raoul's enraged and turns to Javier. 'Who the fuck did you call?'

Chuck laughs, 'Great joke!' whilst Maria and Olivia toast Carla with their tea, who's clenching her teeth through the worst possible betrayal of her oldest possible friend. Shakespeare had always been Bode's favourite, from when she was a child; she should have known Bode would play such a coup one day.

Javier takes out a little piece of paper from his pocket; it's all scrunched and wet from the snot of his hanky but the number is still visible with the writing, 'Call this AMBULANCE,' followed by a number. At the back though, he can now read something else. 'Professional everyday actors' co-operative in central London. All events welcome.'

11

Julio Cortes, southern male

When I think of our fate as a people, said Julio Cortes, sat facing me at the coffee shop in Cheapside sipping a *Volluto*, I think of the perils of limitless sensuality. Ours is not only a story of man's insatiable thirst for sex though, but of his ignorance too. Because this is definitely who we are, he said. Absolutely. Our chief characteristic. No other trait is as dominant in the average southern male. We are as crude as our pigs. This is what Julio Cortes, branch secretary at a southern bank in London, told me as he munched on a buttered muffin, the clouds moving unhurried outside our window towards the British coast.

Consider us sitting here having this shit coffee. Don't even get me started on this shit coffee, Julio Cortes exhaled. But it was too late because he had already started. We all know we should never pay four pounds for a coffee. And we do this in a place where no single fucking dickhead knows what a good coffee is or how to make it. Other than our fellow southern male, who opened this chain of coffee shops and is now a multimillionaire. He was the last one of us other than me to really know about good coffee but he wouldn't make it here. Here he killed it, rendered it into a relic, Julio Cortes said, his hands around his cup of coffee, bringing it to his big, bristly mouth.

And the pretty girl and boy waiters this fucking southern coffee millionaire inflicts on us? Look around! Julio Cortes urged me. Just look around. These fuckers are not real. They are flimsy carton mock-ups, disrespectful to the original human being, even perverse. They kill the coffee, and from their hands it is almost not worth having. Take the cunt face behind the counter, Julio Cortes continued, his back to her. You could blame her for looking like Naomi Campbell. It's a fucking disgrace! These are not people. These are not coffee souls but fake puppets trying to sell you some stupid dream, he insisted. And the design of this place... he mumbled. Decorators with more ass than brain have desiccated it, making it murderously dull. You will agree with me, said Julio Cortes, that a place serving good coffee needs to feel sour and deviate from good taste. But these fuckers, he explained, pointing unashamedly around him, know nothing about the art of coffee. They murder coffee. They have murdered this bar; it's not a bar. The owner has wanted to invent a new kind of caffè, which is the only thing you can do if you call yourself an innovator of any description. But he has created this place which is diabolically deviant. And now every sucker a mile from Cheapside pretends this is 'the' place for coffee, that this is how they have had coffee all their lives. Even the best southerners. It's a fucking travesty!

I sighed. Julio Cortes was right, I thought. But then again perhaps he wasn't fair. He had been unfair many times before. I had been drinking espresso here, with him, every day for a year now. What about me? I tried to sound indignant that he could so easily insult the entire race of southern males and call us dumb on the basis of lazy coffee-drinking habits. What about me? I said again, to which Julio Cortes glanced at my eyes patiently, putting his hands together over the table like a little boy taking confession. What about you? he finally answered laughingly. I come here every day, I added. With you.

Julio Cortes held my stare. Let's talk about *El Griego*, he said. He seemed to be having a moment of reflection.

So there's you, there's me and there's them, Julio Cortes said as if he was onto something. Then there is a painting by a pupil of *El Griego*.

You know I have forever loved *El Griego*, he admitted almost passionately. But few southern males ever really have. I nodded. Not a single southern fucking male admires *El Griego* like they can't tell good coffee. Every southern male except you and me are so fucking dim-witted they cannot admire his art. And you think I am fucking joking. I am not fucking joking, Julio Cortes said. He had himself told me before how he had come to love *El Griego* during a vulnerable life episode years ago when he lived in a crowded, rodent-ridden house in a poor Madrid neighbourhood.

The pricks! Julio Cortes suddenly shouted and stood up from his chair a little. The *putos*. How I fucking loathe them, he said, shaking his arms close to my head across the table. Years not having told me that the bank owned that fucking painting, he added.

I myself was intrigued to know that our institution invested in art, and I was preparing a line of further questioning but need not have bothered as Julio Cortes was already talking over me, engulfed as he was in his own oratory. The clouds outside our window had momentarily faded and we could enjoy a rare piece of blue London sky despite the narrowness of the street facing us and the tall buildings in close vicinity.

Can there be value to an artwork never shown? Locked in a vault? Instead they will show it, parade it for the benefit of illiterate, wealthy, southern fuckers, Julio Cortes talked on. Naturally. Believe me, Joaquín, when I tell you that our moronic managers at headquarters asked me to invite a set of top assholes on our London lists to a cult exhibition of the work, followed by a dinner for the southern cunts. A gift for their vanity. They wanted them self-deluded that they were the only ones ever able to look at this painting even when they won't admire their countryman's work. As a thank you for their fucking commissions. Thanks to the southern fuckers elite of London. We southern fuckers at our bank thank you all! Did our dickhead bosses hope for an adoring scandalised public? Julio Cortes reclined back, legs wide open, taking a hand to his balls for a few seconds. He was so intoxicatingly vulgar, addictive like the smell of an open sewer.

There was a white room and a column, not even a cylindrical column. Not even a fake Greek or Roman column. Not Doric, Corinthian or Ionic. A rectangular column, he started again. Perhaps a Nordic idea of a column because we southerners are such fuckers we are losing our foothold on the world to people even dimmer than us. Who the hell was the imbecile? Who was the bastard instructed by our headquarters to arrange the showing of this most fucking brilliant painting in London under such poor lighting, in surroundings you would not even want to stay in to finish your kebab? Julio Cortes asked looking at me, but I didn't want to guess. There was a lot of cava though, he assured me. The good cava too because I fucking brought it. But there was no introduction and no curator. Only a leaflet of several pages with vacuous words repeated a number of times, our glorious bank logo all over it, explaining nothing to the southern ignorant fuckers in attendance about the masterwork, because the philistine dickhead of our event manager, also a southerner, had not thought it necessary. Or he had thought that it would not be of interest. Or he or she perhaps didn't think anything at all. They knew nothing about anything. There was a pretty phrase the event manager had paid a thousand pounds to be hand-calligraphied at the front of each and every leaflet though: *Celebrating five hundred years of El Griego,* next to a photo of a slick couple of motherfucking businessmen holding a martini, one our thirsty knucklehead clients in formal suits ready for a free party would identify with. Really? Who were the slick fuckers in that photo? They could have been Posh Spice and her husband for all I knew! said Julio Cortes. There were the dinner invitation details my secretary had provided on the back too. The event manager had misspelt the name of the restaurant, hardly unexpected, or perhaps it was my own secretary, the request having arrived only three days before, on my birthday, when she had been preoccupied with covering my office floor in damning red heart-shaped balloons. Another ignorant race, keen secretaries... Julio Cortes downed his cold espresso, making a spiteful face.

And the title of the painting? he asked next. The original title had been *Souls Burning in Hell* not *Burning of the Witches*! Julio Cortes shouted aggrieved. The oil blobs were male! They were male fuckers just like us. All male. Southern ignorant fucking pigs, smearing their faeces on their faces, surrounded by crumbling waste. But not even such vivid scenes were able to start an inner monologue in heads as empty as those of our whoring clients, Julio Cortes added. What was the champagne was all they wanted to know. One even demanded a drink with white spirit. Another spit something trivial like, 'All works of art are unfinished.' The fucker. Ignorant lamebrains couldn't even tell good cava and deserved a vomit of morality thrown upon them, whilst they whispered viciously in business language about their targets and monies as they sipped circling the master painting. Nobody – believe me, Joaquín, when I say NOBODY – looked once at the painting, as they filled their gobs with caviar, truffles, lobster and foie canapés. They were a shore, in full-carousal, waiting for a sea. They were in a playground, on a year out. On a holiday, replicating vain, aimless conversational patterns. Talking water resistance of designer watches. Give plutonium to the fuckers, just finish them off. Let's kill the entire uneducated London-based southerner elite, scorch them down to the earth where they came from. They are unwelcome, this new breed of southerner London thug, hedonist without need for knowledge or life motive. Such a merciless occupying force. To *El Griego*'s ashes. Consign them to the pits of hell to share with cannibals, anarchists and priests. We can't be bound to their shitty amorality. It's not enough to pursue their extinction; our aspiration should be for them to never have been. It was a lovely painting but they would have been happier looking at a pole salvaged from a nearby strip club they hoped to be taken to later, Julio Cortes finished looking more than disgruntled. He could have been such a gentler, hilarious man amongst friendlier company.

Next, Julio asked if I wanted another hideous coffee and I agreed, to hear his story to the end.
    But this is not even the worst, Julio Cortes said when he came back with two more espressos and another muffin for him and

sat back in front of me. The lack of interest for the painting is not even the worst of it, Joaquín. The worst is their salaciousness, he offered. Have you ever been confronted first-hand with the southern male's salaciousness? he asked me straight as if I myself did not suffer from it. What I am talking about is the public celebration of our members' pulling power, which can totally obscure how ignorant we are. This is what I am talking about, Julio Cortes elaborated. Because until HE came in with her, everyone safely ignored everything, including the painting, and got on, a minor stain on my heart. But when the biggest motherfucker who had travelled especially down from headquarters that morning made his grand entrance, – Julio Cortes paused and sighed a deep, deep sigh – then the whole thing became a different affair. And you know who is the bullshit cocksucker I'm talking about? He nodded at me and I nodded back. HIM. Once HE had entered, the moron collective found something brilliant to moron around. My painting – Julio suddenly called it his painting as if the painting's real owners had not loved it enough to be their painting – had never stood a chance. Neither had my cava, which for over an hour before had driven their dribbling and mingling. Only HE would be adored, our firm's supreme dickhead, who was to use this event as a marketing opportunity even if he had not once in his life heard of *El Griego*. Julio Cortes explained of his arch-enemy. But he carried his ignorance with panache as the bank's top performer. And his salaciousness? You may ask, Joaquín. You may ask.

I stayed quiet.

He was carrying her by his hand! Elsewhere in the world people have qualities, but we southerners only had them once. We are like Russians with a deep history of literature yet today so intent on burning books. We new southerners of the southern elite care only for women and money, affirmed Julio Cortes. And HE paraded around MY clients, in MY exhibition, MY woman by his hand. He was like a sponge with no head, only euros and testicles. Do you understand what I am saying to you, Joaquín? Do you understand? asked Julio distressed. That if you suggested to him to buy *El Griego*, which he could given the money he makes whilst we earn peanuts, he would laugh out loud. Not an embarrassed laugh but a spontaneous, hearty one from the gut, and she would laugh alongside him. He would be delighted at my mad uproarious idea, said Julio Cortes, yet point out to me that it would clash with some unwarranted photograph of the pope, nude, by his mantelpiece, interfered by a crazily expensive artist, or that he would rather save the wall space for the thinnest screen ever produced to watch football on, big breasts or other morons like him shouting at each other shocking political opinions they don't understand. And he would be so logical in front of my guests, holding HER hand, humiliating me until I felt utterly embarrassed for admiring *El Griego* and wanting him on my wall myself without ever being able to afford it. Joaquín! Julio shouts at me. When HE came in, the client crowd stopped ruminating, stopped not looking at the painting, and looked at him alone, him and his damsel dangling from his arm. Ignorance and salaciousness is all it takes to mesmerise southern fuckers.

Julio suddenly drew from a hip flask, ten-year-old Oban, he told me, then passed it to me oblivious to the waiter's gaze. I drank. To the morons, the dickheads, the lunatic fucking assholes whom Julio said had fallen for HIM, for his impression of the winner in a commercial, and like grinning clueless tourists had admired Julio's arch-enemy, an arch-successful ape who would never have a heart for *El Griego*. The fucking exhibition was already such a moronic fiasco, Julio Cortes confessed, and there was still the dinner to get through.

You do not need me to point out that *El Griego*, like me, had nothing but hatred for the southern race, Julio Cortes said. Yet here we had a situation where I had facilitated the gathering of this very stupid people to celebrate his painting, to celebrate the man and his school, and the chief imbecile of our institution had invited himself with a trophy pair of tits and was stealing the show. Mindless flabby wankers, nauseatingly self-conscious dickheads all of them, bathing in their own success. What a euphoria of mindlessness as everyone bowed their heads into the new hostess' bust. Fuck client exhibitions. Fuck client perks. I mean fuck them all. And listen to this, Joaquín. Listen to this, Julio Cortes demanded. I still had to take this crowd on to expensively prohibitive Sake no Hana!!! And none of them, none of them had even looked at the painting once, not even for a minute. Did they deserve this? Did I? How I wished HE, the top motherfucker, whoreson, thug of a bitch, unpleasant person, had just gone, gone and taken her away with him so that she couldn't be celebrated anymore. But the lightweight, the ignorant sex beast, typical southerner playboy millionaire was loving it. She's a client, Julio Cortes said he said. A client of his fucking ass, a client of no bank, Julio said. We were supposed to be celebrating *El Griego*, not the top asshole's fucking sexuality, bloody moron, Julio Cortes repeated indignantly, and I suddenly felt waves full of clouds rushing back against our window.

Julio Cortes sat silent for a while after that, in front of me, looking at the London sky. We had both finished our second coffees.

Julio's story was nearing the end. I thought of all the time Julio Cortes had spent outside his country and the hatred he still held for his own people, which consumed him like an obsession become so chronic it was an integral part of who he was.

Unexpectedly, there was a renewed roar of the coffee machine at the back of our table as a queue had formed and was being attended to. We remained seated and Julio started again, talking of the waddling pricks, the chortling little swines of the southern race. Will I tell you what I did? he said to me. I will tell you what I did. I did take them all as arranged to the famous Japanese restaurant, in a tidy single file like stupid little children. One of the guests had seized an unfinished bottle of cava and carried it with him down the road – can you believe it, Joaquín? – and not one, not one fucker thanked me for *El Griego*'s painting, taken out of that secured vault and brought all the way from our headquarters for them to enjoy. None of them thanked me, for having unwillingly witnessed the horror alongside the magnificent. Nor did I thank the organisers for the poor way they had chosen to display the painting. I had the feeling that like the other poor bastards they didn't care. What a theatre of southern idiocy! And at Sake no Hana's private room I sat them all like in *The Last Supper*. She by HIM. She was naturally the only woman at the table and he loved how they all looked at her. And so did she. How they all would have liked a rave full of cheap girls to fulfill their lecherous half-thoughts amongst mingled smells of many vaginas. It was no company for a woman of breeding, amongst a parade of cockerels set on disregarding women except as mothers or whores. Better for my woman to have been alone living eccentrically in some woods on magic mushrooms; or in an insane asylum; an abandoned electricity plant; a deserted warehouse or forsaken docks. So I made it my business to wreck that dinner the best I could, admitted Julio Cortes. Believe me, Joaquín, when I tell you that I fucked the fuckers. I walked amongst them, stupid cretins, and stopped at the woman by my motherfucking colleague, asked her whether she had enjoyed the *El Griego* painting as she stared at me in bewilderment and terror, eyes petrified with confusion because she had finally recognised me. Her lovely hair smelled of lemons. HE next to her smiled a content smile. He was such a prick he could not understand anything. After a bit he said, I think you'd better leave to sort the order out, and he looked at me in the eye. What the fuck! said Julio Cortes, recollecting the incident. What the flying fuck, Joaquín! I went back to my seat at the head of the table and called the head waiter. I would lynch them back, this vulgar mob. A black day for the bank, a black day for true southerners, a black day for the whole male race and a black day for me, Julio Cortes said. How I wish they would all crumble into the sea, he insisted.

Then he stood up again, slightly gripping the table, and I looked alarmed at his face. I told the waiter, Julio said. I told them all. No sushi. No fine wine or champagne. Only beer. Only edamame and beer, fuck you all, ignorant pricks! It was my office budget. It was me hosting, Julio Cortes said almost on fire. It was me paying. If they didn't even know how to admire a fucking master then it was just beans and beer. And they all laughed and cheered as if I was offering sausages to a hungry mass at the end of a toga party and kept talking animatedly amongst themselves and looking at my woman's tits, as if they helped them climb down some erotic ladder into a craved forbidden underworld, and sparing no thought at all for *El Griego*'s painting of souls on fire. But my enemy knew. HE knew what I thought of them all, Julio Cortes said moving against the back of his seat. And I sat at the head of that table sad and alone, searching for a sanctuary in the face of the abyss, remembering the nights I had had with my woman, Ana, and imagining what she would later that night share with the stupid fucking alpha-moron, and how he would come inside her with a howl, his dick glistening like a proud monolith. The chief prick of our bank. The more I thought of his dick, the smaller my own felt. What have they done to me? Julio asked. What have they done to me, Joaquín? What the fuck is going on, Joaquín?

I turned away to face the window again and questioned whether I saw in Julio a vision of my own future, whether he had come into me and my heart was now hardened, my tongue filthy and my eyes faded grey. Neither of us spoke for a time then Julio Cortes hesitated. I did my best, he said, but when I look back at it I feel as if I haven't achieved anything. I hate it all. He seemed calmer after saying that. This work, he said, this success means nothing, nothing at all. This life means nothing. We all self-mutilate for long then walk, run, straight into the flames. We don't heal but burn in the flames of *El Griego* and every hurt lasts forever, Julio assured me, neither raging nor afraid. Ana, Ana, he mumbled, the only one I will not forget, Joaquín. There is nothing I did not give her. Fuck it all. The rest, fuck it all. Fuck it all, he said. Fuck it all, as he pushed a blank letter of resignation to me, a fellow southern male, his only friend and the most senior banker after him in our London office. I leave the world as I found it, he last promised me. I am tired of being strong for other people who have forgotten what life is supposed to be. But I don't want to become tolerant of mediocrity either; I don't want to give them what they want, those things without meaning... To be the strong one is so lonely, he told me. I may as well drink myself to death in the solitude of a cardinal robe, pausing only to fuck real dirty whores and create bitter, monstrous works, like *El Griego*, out of mad thoughts flitting through the sad chambers of my mind.

12

MENTAL

'It's MENTAL,' that's the name she said.

We were sat on the narrow bench that runs along the south wall of the main school building, by the entrance, waiting for our children. 'That is an original business idea,' I said back to her.

She insisted she had built a library of up to ten thousand volumes in her detached three-storey mansion in front of Bute House where you probably needed racing scooter boards just to reach the bathrooms; all classified in alphabetical order, by illness. And at the heart of this grand room she celebrated the oldest DSM manual known to be in existence, as if it were the Magna Carta. She had acquired it from some rare books trader in Texas.

'I know the DSM by heart. It's my Bible.' She brought her bony hand to her heart as if to stop it coming out of her ribcage. A red-haired little girl, she must have been in Reception, passed us by, rolling a bright-orange hula hoop. 'I have no fewer than five students working for me at the moment, all Oxbridge,' she added, keen on keeping the conversation from extinguishing. 'I'm Cambridge, you see, so I have a soft spot.' She crossed both hands on her knees and pointed her toes inside her ballerinas then lifted her feet slightly up from the floor and let them fall again. 'It helps,' she said as I watched.

'Did you read medicine at Cambridge?' I felt obliged to ask.

'Not at all.' She kept moving her feet, repeating the same routine over and over. 'Modern and medieval languages, then went into property management. A Russian fund.' She said that's how she had made her money and met her husband, an ex-banker with an Irish family restaurant downtown where he had been shot age eight on the arm for resisting a robbery. 'Nothing to do with mental health; I'm self-taught in that department,' she insisted.

I nodded, impressed on many counts, for her and her husband. Some people go from butcher to club manager. She had gone from medieval languages to Russian property to mental health, through a husband shot in the arm at an Irish family restaurant.

'Though language skills always help. And I get these young boys, medical students themselves, out of term time. I offer lodging and expenses.'

I thought back to her mansion of tens of rooms, a young medical Oxbridge lad behind each door. 'Kind of fun,' I smiled.

'Even they tell me what I give them to edit is too hard, that they don't understand it themselves. I would need PhDs or experienced real-life professionals to simplify the stuff before it goes online, but they would be too boring. I will get a couple of famous endorsements before we launch, of course. For now, though, I like taking care of the boys.'

'It seems like a great arrangement,' I insisted but she looked at me with some hesitation. Did I truly get her or was I mocking her? I'm not an idiot, her look said.

'It's good to have people around the house.' She had decided to trust me. 'And it's in their contracts to help with my own boys too.' She had two boys the age of my girl, in her same class. 'Oscar is never there and the boys need male figures around them.'

Oscar must have been her husband I guessed though it seemed hardly an Irish name.

'Our house is so big. Loneliness seems to hide around every corner,' she was going soft. 'It's like we invite it and then need to fight it.'

I agreed with a nod again, as I heard a nearby mother whispering that the Year 4s would be late from sports, which panicked me slightly. I felt stuck. 'I would love to see your library one day,' I claimed. 'I have always been interested in mental health but never had time to learn about it. I think it would open a new world for me,' I lied.

'You can't believe how much is out there.' Her face lit up with my interest. 'Anger, panic, bipolar, borderline personality disorder, body dysmorphic disorder, depression, dissociatives, hypomania…' She went through the list as if it were the contents of Ali Baba's cave. 'And don't get me started on drugs and alcohol, don't get me started on eating disorders. OCD, paranoia, phobias…' She sounded utterly jubilant.

I next realised how she looked dangerously thin. I must have always unconsciously assumed it was her choice of jeans leggings. 'Does reading about all this stuff not confound you to imagine you have it?' I wasn't exactly calling her a deranged fabulist…

'Never.' She knew her mind.

'I think I'm too much of a hypochondriac, that I would convince myself that I suffer from every disease after I have read the symptoms,' I murmured, explaining myself.

'Well, we all do. I have so far identified two or three favourites for myself.'

Had she not just said 'Never'?

'It's changed my life, knowing,' she assured me. 'It's nothing to do with being confounded into believing,' she was clarifying. And I wondered if she was expecting me to probe further. It seemed a dangerous game...

I stayed quiet and hoped it was not psychosis she had identified for herself. Or schizoaffective disorders. She could be hallucinating that I was her new best friend and next decide to kill me.

'And I have helped many acquaintances with my work, especially women. I mean, don't get me started on postnatal. I mean who on earth wouldn't go mad after what we women have to go through!' She was whispering too close to my face. 'Or post-traumatic. How are you expected to feel when you announce to your jerk of a husband you know he's sleeping with his secretary and all he manages in reply is to put his knife and fork together over his new helping of dauphinoise, staring powerless across the table whilst you keep crying?' She winked at me as if she welcomed murder and bloodshed to bring women enlightenment, because husband love would never push us beyond the onion peeler. 'Those poor women!' she sighed. Of course nothing she was saying had anything to do with me or her specifically.

I had to reassure myself this woman was only another mum entrepreneur, trying to promote her services amongst other mums. She was selling her MENTAL and I shouldn't try to unearth any alternative hidden meanings in what she was saying. But there was something that had been bothering me all along...

Actually, two things. First, I realised I had never seen her without her hat; perhaps she wore unbrushed hair parted as if it was curtains and felt pressured to cover it in glamorous company; her choice of look was definitely unusual for a cool mum. Maybe it was driven by a recent peculiar brash with non-mainstream fashion, drugs or religion. I had never thought about it, like the skinny legs under her leggings. And then there was a strange, almost spasmodic movement to her hand, every so often.

'Tardive dyskinesia,' she said, almost proud that I had noticed it.

A chill went up my spine.

She handed me her business card, holding it with both her hands as if we were in a tea ceremony or she thought it may fly in the wind. 'I am sure you would find my advice useful too,' she said.

'Sure. I will definitely have a look at the website once it's up.' I cursed Mr Smith, the sports teacher, for failing to keep to his schedule.

My apparent willingness to play ball with her though, had clearly made her beam, and after a short silence she started again. She knew I had no escape.

'The site will go through all the usual culprits,' she smiled. 'Take loneliness. It's a vicious cycle. Feeling lonely damages your mental health and your mental health then makes you feel more lonely. You have to think. Think about what is making you lonely. It's not good for you to sit alone at home all day!' She was sounding like my mother. 'Regularly check how you are feeling. Make new connections. Open up to people, like me.' She had her arms wide open but couldn't hide her right hand convulsing again, fretting like a lunatic limb. 'Take it slow though,' she advised caution, then bent forward until the rim of her hat touched the side of my face. She was whispering her warning in my ear and I felt unexpectedly aroused; she had a great storytelling voice. 'Be careful when comparing yourself to others. Everyone has their own way to be occupied. You don't want any more children? Get a lover.' She was succeeding in terrifying me.

I decided to laugh to break her spell. A powerful roar that to everyone else waiting for their kids in the courtyard must have sounded like a cry for help. But nobody came to rescue me. They all ignored me and went back to their own worlds. I was alone. With her.

'Another big stressor is the money thing,' she stated authoritatively, thankfully stepping back from my ear. 'Worrying about money,' she explained.

She had lost me there. She was rich, everybody knew. Did she think I was less better off and she could teach me?

'For me it's dealing with the monthly Amex bill and how my husband gets things wrong all the time.'

I almost sighed and then turned it into the usual nod.

'"Keep a diary of your spending," he cries to me. "Try and record what you spent and why!"' Her impersonation of her husband was funny. 'We also keep a log of our moods around bill-time, but nothing has helped us so far work out any triggers or understand more about our behaviour. I know we will though, that we will eventually hit the nail on the head.' She seemed confident in their resolve.

'I see,' I told her even when I didn't, if I was truly lost for words. Of course, in a way she was right and sensible but she was also totally crazy. Was she not? And I had no clue what she wanted of me.

'You have to retain control.' She raised her voice, her spastic hand secured to my knee. 'Or you will give into the phobias, become obsessive. I've seen it all. Women prisoners of house dust, constantly cleaning, hoovering. Obsessive ironing. Households where the washing machine gets no rest, not even on Sundays.'

It was the stuff of nightmares being gunned from her mouth and I looked around for help again, but nobody seemed to notice us.

'A woman in deep fear of the metal hooks her husband produced to hang *jambon*,' she continued. 'Another horrified by rushing water; a young girl whose terror of bullets from her father's hunting rifle introduced her to Jesus no less!'

Did she really keep such company!

She let my knee go eventually and reclined back against the school wall, rumpling the back of her hat, her image embodying an urn of phobias itself, mixed with all the nervous smiles and tears of her patients, as she mumbled to the sky still talking to me. 'My crew of actors are brilliant, brilliant at playing it all out in front of my clients, to show them right to their faces how ridiculous they are. Because life like that will not do. It just will not do!'

I feared that she was working herself up into a frenzy and I would not like to be held responsible for whatever she did when she went back home in an anxious, raging mess.

'Check out the videos on my website as soon as it's up.' She pointed to her business card still in my hand.

'I will,' I promised her as convincingly as I could.

'It's as easy as those tests you take in magazines, guiding you with questions to find out your fate. It's even easier.'

'Sure,' I said.

There was a welcome silence.

After a round of heavy breathing to the rhythm of her ballerina feet routine again, she leaned forward from the wall and looked at me once more.

'Then you call me and we can help.'

I wanted to cry inside but it would only make her right that something was wrong with me.

'My master breather can make you focus on your inhales, help you picture yourself somewhere serene,' she added.

I had been serene before she had arrived.

'My house environment is tested,' she sounded convinced she knew what she meant.

'Tested for what?' I asked softly, almost to myself.

'We can listen to the right music together,' she urged, excited. 'My library has chant tapes from monks all across Asia. You do Pilates, right?'

'Once a week?' I blatantly lied.

'We need to take that up a notch,' she said, disapproving of my laziness. 'And we can also get creative. I have a mud studio, and a woman comes in twice a week from Ghana.'

I nodded on automatic and immediately blamed myself. She was taking all my nodding as confirmation of commitment to her cause. 'I prefer the outdoors for relaxation,' I courageously added to defend myself from her intrusions.

'I couldn't agree more.' She gave me reason for once. Then her body stepped back an inch from mine on the bench, as if I had hurt her. 'That's why we got a dog,' she told me out of the blue. 'I jog him every lunchtime around our gardens.' Next she took her mobile out of a little expensive-looking handbag in the shape of an old-fashioned school satchel and settled for tech time.

My chance to escape!

But as soon as I made the motion to get up from the bench, she put her phone back in her satchel and started again.

'I have my app-time strictly curtailed, you see. We are virtually a tech-free home, happily pushing my husband and his work out onto the front porch!' She smiled, hiding her previous hurt. 'Less tech, more sleep is my mantra.' She tapped her hand on the bench and I was unsure whether it was convulsing or she was asking me to sit back down.

I sat back down.

'You should try Selfridge's new sleep class! It's the only one in the UK. Have you heard of The Sleep Wheel?' she was again addressing me in Punjabi, Sanskrit, some illuminating language barred from my vocabulary.

'I just sleep at home...' I sounded in doubt when I should have been dead certain of what I did and how right it was.

She looked at me disappointed though, again. 'It's not just a fad,' she said. 'Can I ask, how do you relax before you go to bed?' For an instant she didn't look real but like a wax figurine, a strange alive person but a soulless object too.

'I read a book?' Was that too obvious?

'You should meet my masseur!' She smiled. 'Now, a night after him, that is a good night's sleep!' She winked at me like before. 'And it's not like any fucker can do it, just him,' she added without excusing her swearing, as if it was the word of The Lord. 'And make sure where you sleep is comfortable.' She was offering me the full set of advice, live, and I couldn't stop her. 'John and I have invested heavily in a good mattress, although he mostly sleeps elsewhere.'

I thought her husband's name was Oscar?

She winked again. 'And keep a sleep diary.'

'It's a high-maintenance process,' I finally protested. 'Wow! A lot of stress. Not enough hours in the day.'

'You will see it takes stress away,' she stressed the stress and the away bits, 'so you can rest like a baby. And a good sleep means a tranquil mind, which helps you maintain emotional resilience.' She had obviously researched the topic well. 'Because you cannot, for the love of God, understand how emotional resilience helps.'

I was back to nodding.

'If my child forgot his lines at the school play or could not make a sound at his trumpet recital, it would have made me cry a year ago. But now...' she was doing her ballerina feet routine again, 'it's just a drop in the ocean.'

Her mobile pinged inside her handbag, offering me a moment of respite.

'The kids are still fifteen minutes away,' she informed me reading her message.

I cringed and glanced at the demonic red digits of my cheap wristwatch.

I tried to step away for the second time, but she offered me something from a little silver sachet she had taken out of her bag when she went to put her phone back in.

'Himalayan salt almonds,' she explained. 'People just don't know how important food is, how it affects your mental health.' She munched. 'You go to the gym for your body, your face even nowadays. The face gym in Harvey Nics takes years off you! But what about your brain? If you do not have your brain working, you have nothing.'

She was exhausting.

'What about your brain?' she asked me directly. 'Have you ever lost your brain?'

I felt momentarily raped but recovered quickly. 'I feel I lose my brain every day,' I joked nervously.

'So did I. But then you need help,' she told me curtly. 'Do you eat enough fruit? Do you eat enough meat?'

I needed to get bolder with her or she would eat me alive. 'I have enough wine I guess,' I laughed again. But I was not helping myself.

'It's no laughing matter,' she told me off. 'I don't touch that stuff, not any more. It's evil.'

I felt hurt, scolded like a naughty nursery child. I wondered whether she hoped her pristine brain would be preserved in a bowl and displayed to be admired in her own purpose-made museum, or perhaps passed on to a next generation of superhumans, or trialled on aliens in a parallel universe, to make them more intelligent. She was starting to get to me.

'Vegetables and fruit contain a lot of the minerals, vitamins and fibre we need to keep us physically and mentally healthy.'

She was so full of unhelpful tips. She was worse than those American channels where every bloody ad is for pharmaceuticals. I started feeling sick, strived to panic about the modern world.

'And keep yourself hydrated,' it was an order. 'Or you may find it difficult to concentrate or think clearly.'

I tried to smile.

'You might also start to feel constipated, which puts no one in a good mood. Herbal tea is best.'

I hadn't had tea in my lifetime despite years living in this country; I thought it for losers and the Indians. I wanted to tell her I was a three-espressos-a-day kind of woman. Perhaps I was intent on killing myself? But I kept my neutral smile for her, given laughing things off hadn't worked before.

'And the right fats! Nuts, especially almonds, seeds, avocados, milk, yoghurt, cheese and eggs. Plus enough protein to help the chemicals in your brain regulate your feelings; Cowshed's quinoa is best.'

I couldn't tell her how many of the things on her list I would have served only to donkeys. I didn't eat seeds. What was quinoa again? And I abhorred cowdung's (or whatever its name) health spa; it was so overpriced.

'Then feel your gut. Just feel your gut!' she was shouting, enlightening me like an apostle his disciples, in the middle of the school courtyard. She was closing in on me but still nobody came to help, everyone ignored us when they must have surely noticed us centre stage. 'Just please, feel your gut. Your state of mind is closely connected to your gut. Your gut communicates with your brain. It will tell your brain you should kill your alcohol. You should kill your caffeine. Caffeine is a stimulant. Having too much caffeine can make you feel anxious and depressed, disturb your precious baby sleep.'

'Are we allowed to have any fun?' It took all my valiance to interrupt her, even if I still tried to sound amused rather than confrontational.

'Choose at your own peril.' She definitely couldn't take a joke. 'One needs to be mindful to feel great, to find happiness.

Mindfulness can help you increase your awareness of your thoughts and feelings, to manage unhelpful thoughts, develop more helpful responses to difficult events. Be kind towards yourself!'

I definitely thought I was being kind to myself every evening when I put our girl to bed and poured myself a bucket of Ott.

'You need to feel good if you are to be able to manage unhelpful thoughts,' she was mumbling to herself, 'to deal with life's assholes...' She suddenly seemed miles away. 'Like when I worked in the camps at Calais,' she said full of her own memories.

'You worked in the refugee camps?' What other camps could she mean in Calais? It was a complete flip and I was totally unexpectedly in awe of this woman. No. I was confounded, like I could not square things up anymore. And I felt guilty I had eroded any good in her almost from the start in my mind, disallowing her of an opportunity to be trusted, when perhaps I should have listened to her openly. Willingly.

I could see the kids arriving at the school gates.

'Just don't get obsessive about things,' she said casually as she got up from the bench, as advice for the road. 'But think. Think and prepare.' She put her hands on my shoulders once I had stood up myself. 'It's a battle. Everyone needs to find their way through it. Build their own ballet barre to prevent the fall.'

Next she disappeared, a thin shade with a hat on top, through the fog of the courtyard.

13

Luck of the draw

They are mother and daughter by the kitchen table against the main wall with the window. The table is Formica, pale blue; a shade called Cadet, Ana, the daughter, seems to remember. She asked for the table to be sent to London after her grandmother died. Her grandmother had been a great cook and the 'shitty' table, as they all called it, was the centrepiece of her kitchen. Ana had cut her fingers more than three times and burnt her right hand as a kid on that table. When Ana's dad had started earning well, he had offered to buy his mother-in-law a proper wooden table, but she had refused. The Formica pale-blue Cadet had stayed.

'*Galletitas de nata* (cream cookies).' Ana's eyes still fill with tears every time she takes the recipe out. *At least something that stands up to time*, she thinks. Her mother has borrowed an apron and it looks a bit too tight on her.

'I would not have thought you could get fresh milk anymore, not in a big city like this,' Ana's mother is surprised. Since her husband died she comes to stay with Ana for a month every year, but every time, everything seems different to her.

'It's a new service I found on the net,' explains Ana. 'The farm is within the M25. People here rave about reducing their carbon footprint.' She doubts her mother understands what she's talking about. The good thing for Ana is that the fresh milk is delivered daily in aluminium containers and she can collect and keep the cream depositing on the surface until she has enough for *galletas de nata*, like in the old days.

Ana's mother turns and turns the cookie mix in a big bowl, working her arm muscles. There's sweat on her brow, flab floats under her nude arms and her hands look almost cadaverous around the big wooden spoon.

'Carlos has stopped talking,' says Ana.

'Has he now?' Ana's mother is not taking the news too seriously. Ana's brother has hardly talked to her in the past year. Not even in the past ten years. He had a big brawl with his father way before he died and she didn't stand up for him at the time. But even after her husband's death, Carlos has not come back to her; it's a splinter in her heart but she's resigned by now.

'He finally went to see Aunt.' Ana is talking of her mother's sister.

'I thought he never would after their fall-back.' Ana's mother knows her son has a need to fight everybody but has ceased to blame herself for it.

'He said he wanted to see her before she died.' Ana remembers how her brother had never gone to visit their dad in his final days, and she knows how poignant it is for them all. She puts the oven on and takes a tray out of the cupboard. 'The mix will soon be ready.'

'Did he go alone?' Ana's mother still worries for Carlos more than for any other of her children. Despite his hungry fists, she knows deep down he is the most vulnerable one, that he was never right in his head.

'With Pili.' Ana calls Carlos's wife Pili although everyone else calls her Pilar. 'And the kids,' she adds.

'He took the kids?' Ana's mum almost drops her bowl, startled. She thinks it irresponsible of Carlos to take his kids on a visit to a dying aunt they hardly know. But she does not want to argue so she hides her disapproval. 'How are the kids?' she enquires.

Ana's mother has not seen her son's kids once this year, despite living in the same small town as them. She can't believe she has to come all the way to London, to her daughter, to get news of her own son and grandchildren who live in her home town. The world is crazy, but it is what it is.

'Alicia was the only one who went in, I think.' Ana always hated the name Alicia but she never told Carlos, of course; he would have taken it the wrong way. Carlos often takes things the wrong way. He's prone to rage. But Alicia was the name of their mother's other sister who died young and Ana had not wanted it for her daughters, nor for her nieces really.

'I meant how they are doing generally,' Ana's mum clarifies. 'I have not seen them in months.' She sounds possibly accusatory but Ana ignores her.

'The other girls waited outside, that's what Pili told me.'

'How old is Alicia now?' Ana's mother can never keep track of her grandchildren's ages. She has ten grandchildren all together, and at seventy she thinks her confusion is justified. 'Twelve?' she tests herself. 'It must have been hard for her.'

Ana takes the bowl from her mother's hands and walks to the oven tray. She lowers her gaze over the kitchen table. 'I can do the shapes now. Have a seat, Mum. Take off your apron.' She waves her mother up the steps where the small kitchen opens into an even smaller living room, to her favourite armchair. She can still see her and talk to her from the kitchen table; London houses are so compact...

But there is only silence for a few minutes.

'You haven't been to see her yet,' a voice travels from the burgundy velvet armchair.

Ana's mother hasn't asked a question. It's a statement. Perhaps not even a statement. Ana thinks it's probably a reproach that she has not travelled to see her aunt since she was admitted to hospital. 'No, I have not,' she admits.

She continues setting blobs of mix on the oven tray by the kitchen table but her heart is thumping. She could claim that she's busy with the kids' schools, or that it's difficult to get time to travel from London. But she would be lying. Why should she want to lie about her own frailties, her own fears, to her own mother?

'I already told you, Mum. I can't face seeing her how Carlos saw her. She was such a strong lady, so proud of her brio.' Ana feels too weak. She's holding back tears from over-flooding her eyes. 'I'd rather just look at that picture.' She raises a hand to point at a little acrylic portrait Ana made of her favourite aunt, Warhol-style, hanging on the wall where the kitchen opens into the living room, 'She won't recognise me if I visit anyway.'

Ana, still pouring mix over the tray in the kitchen, has composed herself from the heart thumps and the tears, and is looking at her mother facing her own sister's portrait.

She suddenly turns to Ana. 'So, what did your brother tell you exactly?' she asks. 'Before he went quiet, I mean...' She almost sounds scornful.

And Ana thinks how she can't quite read her. But if she had to put her money on it, she would say her mother's look spells pity, for her. For her brother.

'He said when he walked into her room, the smell was so bad he retched,' Ana answers after an instant of hesitation. Today she's intent on talking about things as they are. There has been enough pussyfooting around her family in the past and she does not welcome it anymore.

But she's taken by surprise by her mother's roaring laugh. It makes her jump and miss her pouring; *this one cookie will look more like a splat than a perfect circle. Damn!*

'And we are so lucky she's there. You can't imagine the other places she could have ended up in!' Ana's mother tells Ana once she stops laughing.

Ana feels uncomfortable. 'He said he wished he hadn't gone, that he could have kept that memory of the last three-course meal Aunt had cooked him to perfection of cheese soufflé, tender rabbit and gateaux Basque.' It had been Ana's aunt and not her mother who had learnt the art of cooking from Ana's grandmother.

Ana's mother laughs again. She really has useless children, she thinks, but then it is what it is.

'So, how is Aunt then, Mum?' Ana sounds almost angry at her mother's sense of humour.

Ana's mother turns dead serious: it's her chance to spare nothing. *But what good would it do?* she thinks. 'Well, I visit her once a week to bring her new clothes,' she explains.

Ana nods.

'I take her old clothes away in a large plastic bag provided by the nursing home. I carry it myself to the laundry across the road, even if it's heavy.'

Ana has put the cookies in the oven and sets the timer. She's already regretting having got her mum talking about her aunt.

'I used to get a car waiting for me to take me to a cheaper laundry farther away,' Ana's mother looks set in stone, 'but the driver complained of the smell of the clothes, even through the thick refuse bag, and I was too embarrassed to bother him again the next time.'

Ana comes up the two steps separating the living room from the kitchen. The split level makes the room feel bigger. She sits on an identical armchair, a shade lighter, a step from her mum and thinks to take her hand but she's suddenly self-conscious. No. She's scared. She sees the black void again and the plunge ahead of her and knows she can't panic now. Instead, she tries to change conversation.

'I got these new chairs at Dwell. They copy all the famous designs for less. You like them?' She caresses the velvet on the arm of her chair with the same hand she had thought of using to hold her mum's.

'Yes, Ana,' her mum is toneless. 'Their wine colour is divine.'

Ana smiles at her.

'At least she's using her clothes now.' Ana's mother is back talking about her sister.

'What do you mean?' asks Ana.

'Well, she's changing every day.'

Ana doesn't understand.

'For the first three weeks at that home, your aunt went on strike,' her mother explains.

'What do you mean, Mum?'

'She was so angry I had put her there that she was not changing her clothes; she stayed the whole day in her nightie. Can you imagine your proud aunty, going around the home, even the garden, uncleaned, in her nightie all day long?'

Ana can't.

'She used her oldest nightie too, out of spite. She looked a mess.'

'You didn't put her there, Mum,' Ana clarifies.

'At least the last times I visited she was dressed. Last week it was that nice blouse in Liberty print you had sent her years ago.'

Ana can't believe her mother is doing this to her. But she knows her mother probably can't believe Ana is doing this to her own mother.

'Although she was wearing it the wrong way round. The nurses had not even told her!'

'Did you tell them?'

'It's worse if you complain. But I have learnt to check that she's wearing panties when I am there. That would be too much. Serious neglect. I would have to say something then.'

'I see,' Ana is lost for words and she feels the tears coming up again.

'And visiting is not the worst,' Ana's mother sighs. 'You can't believe the paperwork. To cut off the services at her home she's not using anymore, one almost needs to go to the companies themselves and cut off the heads of their executives.

'It's unbelievable!' Ana's mum sounds despairing.

But Ana knows her mum is a fighter. And then, at least this gives her something to do after the death of Ana's dad. Of course, caring for her sister must not be easy from an emotional point of view but then her mother was never too emotional. Ana frets she's only making excuses for herself and sees the black void again.

'If you knew the trouble I'm going through to prepare her space at the cemetery!' Ana's mum exclaims full of outrage as if she had just been told the price of onions in the market has doubled.

'Do you want some tea, or a glass of sherry, whilst we wait?' Ana desperately needs a glass of *manzanilla*.

Ana's mother will join her. She goes down to the fridge and pours two *manzanillas* then comes back to her chair by her mother.

Ana's mum chin-chins with her daughter and, for a second, Ana feels elated, as if they were truly celebrating something, even if it was only being together. She hates how, in recent years, any limited time they spend side by side has to be wasted talking about someone dying. 'You will see it's normal when you reach my age,' Ana's mum had told her a few years ago, but she still fights it.

'I saw you have that Calèche in the guest bathroom,' Ana's mum tells her sounding curious.

'Yes, those are the bottles Aunty gave me every year. Because she thought I should wear her same perfume, Granny's perfume. Granny had given them to me every Christmas and then Aunty started doing it after Granny died.'

'But they are unopened?'

'Yes, I never had the heart to tell her that I don't like it. I never used it. I used it when Granny was still alive but then I couldn't anymore.'

Ana's mother throws a look to her daughter as if she were stupid. Ana is sure her mother thinks she's weak, impractical and hopeless. But she can't confront her to explain herself.

'I take one to your aunt every time I visit. It's the only thing that gives her pleasure nowadays…' Ana's mother speaks, pensive. 'Can I take down yours when I leave? You don't want them anyway.'

Ana remains silent. The cookies beep and she runs to them, almost relieved. 'Three more minutes,' she shouts from the kitchen, a wave of heat from the open oven burning her face, then moves the timer.

When Ana's back at her chair, her mum looks plain angry and it reminds her of when she was little and had done something terribly wrong, bad enough for her mother's trademark pinch-&-twist; it used to hurt like hell.

'I get it,' Ana's mum says. 'You want to forget your aunt is dying like your brother forgot that your dad was sick.'

Ana feels terrible, mid that plunge into the black void; if she weren't seated she knows she would lose her balance. And she suddenly feels like puking. This could be a fight like that between Dad and Carlos. It could be irreparable. She swallows hard.

'So does Carlos. Everybody does. Mind you, your aunty tries to forget she's dying herself.' Ana's mum laughs her odious laugh again.

Ana still doesn't say anything. She wants to say something like 'it's so complicated'; 'with the kids I am swamped'; 'I have no help in London'; and 'I feel I need to be strong for them, look to the future, that I cannot dwell in the past, I cannot afford to become sad or emotional'. She constantly feels she's living in a world with no patience to hear anyone out. And her mother would reply that she used to have them and care for her own mother and all the rest. But not everyone is as strong. 'What good does it do to be strong anyway? Aunt was strong and look at her now. Does it change anything?' Ana has said it aloud.

'Well, she never exactly sacrificed for anything or anybody out of a sense of rightness or duty. She was only determined to always do what she wanted!' Ana's mum starts laughing again.

Ana is unsettled by such a description of her aunt (which she knows is accurate) and by her mum's laughing. But at least it diffuses the sense of confrontation between them, as if the cruelty welled in her mum a minute before had subsided.

'I'm surprised she hasn't tried to run away, from the home?' Ana attempts to join her mum in seeing the funny side of it, away from her black hole.

'Well, in the first days, the nurses found she packed every night and hid her luggage under the bed, ready for her flight.' Ana's mum is holding Ana's stare and both their sets of eyes look vulnerable.

'Yes, Carlos told me they told him.' Ana remembers she is worried about Carlos.

'At least she doesn't do that anymore,' Ana's mum sounds reassured. 'She even agreed to go to the hairdresser last week, though she probably cancelled at the last minute. She's driving the nurses mad.'

'Carlos felt bad he hadn't talked to her for ten years, for

something as silly as her calling him a bad husband,' Ana exhales. 'But when he asked her to forgive him, she asked him who the hell he was and what was he doing in her room!' Ana doesn't know if Carlos can take these things; he was never totally stable. And Pili tells her he has been on antidepressants for the last three years. They have visited many doctors and nothing has helped. Does it feel like her black void? She hasn't told her mum a word about it.

'I'm sure she was not at all offended with him for not visiting before,' says Ana's mum. 'She doesn't really care. She did mean it when she said she thought your brother a weak loser and that he could not even care about his appearance enough to please his wife.' She hides a sneer with her hand. 'You know Aunty. She was ruthless like that and she never really thought about it twice.'

Ana shivers. 'What if Carlos doesn't ever talk again?'

Ana's mother shrugs.

'Pili worries the visit took him over the edge and he can't see the point of life anymore,' Ana is almost pleading. She shouldn't alarm her mother but can't cope with things herself.

'*Chorradas…*' Ana's mum dismisses her, her eyes back to her sister's portrait. 'It's a good portrait!' she adds cheerfully. Then after a few long minutes comes a breakthrough perhaps. 'Would you like me to talk to him?' she's yielding.

Ana's mother's voice leaves an echo of kindness.

The oven beeps again. Ana attends to it.

The cookies are done. She takes the tray out and lets them cool. She goes back to her mum for her glass and refills both their glasses with another sherry.

'Let me tell you a story,' Ana's mum says as they sit side by side with their sherry glasses, the aroma of *galletitas de nata* filling the air.

'I had lunch with my neighbour the week before I travelled here to see you; he's ninety-two years old.'

Ana nods.

'He has been in a wheelchair from age fifty-two, after a hospital mistake during an operation which changed his life.'

Ana frowns.

'He recovered.'

Ana phews.

'He didn't recover. He was reborn. He found a new way to get out of his house. He found a new way to drive. He found a new way to work. He found a new way to live. He buried his wife three years ago and he still goes out, drives, works, lives. He took me to a fantastic restaurant for Sunday lunch. Very elegant.'

'You are not now going to tell me that you are having an affair!' Ana giggles to her mum like a little girl. The *manzanilla* must be getting to her head.

'That's not the point of this story.'

'Okay,' she's blushing.

'We had a phenomenal time and he paid, of course.' Ana's mum would not have had it any other way. 'He behaved like a total gentleman.' She pauses as if she has finished.

'So what's the point of the story?' Ana can't get it.

'Go fetch me a cookie, we need to see how we did!'

Ana comes running back with four tests cookies, two for each, and feels a déjà vu, as if she had gone back forty years on a good day with her mother alone.

'The point is, life is luck of the draw,' Ana's mother assures her. 'And you can be as scared as you want, and your brother can pout and rage all he wants. But nothing's gonna change. You get what you get. We all do what we can to survive with what life throws at us. And it's just bloody luck of the draw. So don't fret so much.'

They chin-chin, Ana thinking her mum is an Aladdin lamp she is too often too frightened to rub. 'To the cookies,' she says.

'What luck they taste almost like Granny's.'

14

Corporate retreat

She kept shouting, towering by the door outside her glass office in the direction of my cubicle. There were at least seven cubicles in between her office and my spot, and their owners were making themselves invisible.

I saw Belinda lowering her head closer to her keyboard and Jack putting his headphones on. Sato went as far as cowering under his desk because it was in his genetic make-up that he could not stomach confrontation; missing enzymes for it or something. We called him Sato-missing-enzymes, and Sato was only his surname. I had no idea what his first name was.

This wasn't the first time she had yelled at me, exasperated by my uselessness. But it was certainly the most savage. She was holding the report I had given to her and started quoting from it. Amongst all the other faults in my report, I had missed a date in the calendar, and one of her *telefonia* companies in Bogotá had released results that had taken her by surprise. I had tried to tell her that the date had been only announced the night before and marked as 'provisional'. But she was right and I was wrong anyway. Day or night, I was still hers and I should have let her know.

Next, she initiated the name-calling: worthless, hopeless,

incapable. I was tits on a bull. I was an ashtray on a motorbike. She was offering them all a circus that could petrify them or they could cherish. When I realised everyone was listening attentively, perhaps even recording her words, yet nobody would stand up for me, I voluntarily fell to my knees, touching the filthy carpet of my cubicle, and sheltered behind my flimsy wall crawling like an insect. I asked for the earth to eat me! It did not and she kept shouting, full of entitlement, as if she understood both the rightness and cruelty of what she was saying. I thought the hurt would hurt forever.

She would refuse to see me again that day but I was busy enough as it was, preparing reports for five other companies expected to announce results that week.

Jack dropped by my desk for gossip that afternoon and we talked of madness, marriage and death. He said I was lucky because women manage helplessness better, it being less embarrassing in a sex the whole terrified man world is hoping will retain some docility for their own sake. Lindsay came for a cup of tea; she asked whether I thought my destiny was to become a saint and we discussed whether that was a possible career path.

I took only one break in the six hours following the yelling episode to go for a pee, and I called my mother from the restroom on my mobile; I had a good cry. Still, my life was too alien for Mum to understand, she who wanted me to go back home and help my dad rear pigs for *chorizo*.

At eleven in the evening I logged in to the bank's system for a cab and went downstairs to wait in line by the taxi queue manager.

'I love your skirt,' the manager said in a flirty tone within the boundaries of acceptability.

'The nicest thing anyone has told me all day.'

He was black, tall and handsome but made to wear a stupid-looking hat. He informed me the bank would soon move the taxi station to the inner courtyard, 'We need to avoid it being so visible to jealous strangers who think bankers are scum and should not enjoy luxuries.' He smiled.

'I think so too.' *I am in the wrong job*, I thought.

The manager laughed and made sure I was allocated a nice pink cab. It cheered me up.

In the cab, I was gagging for a beer and the driver spoke football and the glories of Real Madrid. It happened often when they picked up on my thick Spanish accent.

But I really was not in the mood for football, which I hated even on a good day. At least the driver's constant dribble was like a calming chant and took my mind off things.

At home I rang the bell despite it being late but Rosamie didn't come to the door. Perhaps she had fallen asleep with the kids. My husband would be working for six months from New York and I was a single mum. Or perhaps Rosamie was a single mum and I was a legal entity.

I opened the door with my own keys and took my shoes off by the entrance, hung my coat and walked to the children's room. It was dark in the children's room and it took some time for my eyes to adjust. I reached for my children's bodies on their beds, but could find nothing. Then I realised there was nothing. I felt short of air. Locked out of life.

Next I told myself there had to be a perfectly reasonable explanation. Rosamie was fool-proof. I had interviewed her myself. She had been with me for almost a year now. She had complained about a few things and asked for a raise but I felt all was in hand. I had shouted at her once at breaking point, when she had come to ask for something stupid which did not deserve my attention. But nothing over what my friends told me they yelled to their maids. Had something happened and she had needed to rush away? Why had she not called?

As I reached for my mobile, the doorbell rang.

Suddenly, my kids were in front of me, sleepy-eyed in their pyjamas.

Where was Rosamie? Why had she not called? It was unacceptable. My middle-aged English neighbour I had probably talked to twice in the whole time we had lived here and never liked was handing my kids to me.

'I found them crying this afternoon. I heard them through the wall for ages and got worried enough to call Jon.'

'Jon, the porter?'

I had only met Jon once and we had talked cars and baseball. Or perhaps he had and I had only listened.

'He has all our keys.'

'Where's Rosamie?'

'They had been left alone. The kids say she just left,' my neighbour was telling me looking more serious than death. She was judging me too. It was written all over her face that she thought I was a bad mother. *Malamadre*!

What was written over my own face?

I was flabbergasted but still had the presence of mind to usher the kids back in and tell them to go to their beds, so they would stop hearing the damned conversation.

'They have eaten,' she told me next. 'Fish and chips.'

'Thank you.'

'They seemed very hungry.'

'I just don't understand what happened to Rosamie.'

My neighbour seemed uncomfortable.

'Would you like to come in?' I suddenly realised I had forgotten my manners. 'Please.'

She did not. She was building up her courage to tell me something. 'We didn't call the police this time but would obviously have to if it happens again.'

Did she mean to report me?

Did she mean me?

I closed my door on her face and ran to hug the kids.

I stayed hugged to the kids all night, full of fury and guilt. I tucked my head under the crease of my oldest boy's arm. In his bulk, I felt less empty.

At dawn I texted my husband. I would be handing in my resignation.

He would not respond for another six hours. I should have texted his work phone had I wanted a response, but I hadn't. And I didn't call my mother to tell her either.

Next I checked Rosamie's room. She had truly packed and gone. There was nothing left. No note. And she had not taken anything of ours with her. I could denounce her, but we had not been paying her National Insurance.

At seven I prepared the breakfast and woke the kids up, as if nothing had happened.

Except they knew something had, because I was never there for breakfast. They seemed elated that Mum was walking them to school, and I could not sense any trauma from the night before.

Could kids really bounce back like that, forget in a flash the enormity of what had happened?

Back at home I called work and was connected to my boss, Dragon Lady.

'Where the fuck are you?'

'Stop.'

'Moon Communications results are out and you are nowhere to be seen.' *Thump on a desk.* 'I had to search everywhere for the quarterly templates and your file system is a mess. We even took ten minutes to understand the fucking password. Have I not told you to—'

'Stop!' I yelled. 'I call to resign.'

'What the fuck, I don't have time for this now,' she was walking away.

I thought she was terminating the call but she came back to the phone.

'Call personnel this afternoon after three and talk to Lisa,' she ordered me. 'I have to go now.' She hung up.

The day went slowly.

I ate a can of crab meat from the fridge and had three beers. The boys had clubs until five. At three I called Lisa. Lisa said I had been put forward for the HCT Himalaya Clinic Trip as a 'breakdown situation'.

'Could you explain further?'

'Sarah Biney says you have potential and she doesn't want to lose you,' she made my boss sound like a harvester of good souls.

'Fuck Sarah!' I said to Lisa about Dragon Lady.

'So the way it works is we take you to the Himalayas on a very special trip and mend you,' she insisted.

'I will explain to you the way it works, the way it works is fuck Sarah!' I was enraged my kids could have come to harm because of me and nobody wanted to hear it.

'Sarah is very powerful,' Lisa was persistent, 'and if you want to see the money from your options or even work in your sector ever again, I would not recommend to fuck Sarah.' Lisa was patient and resolute.

'Do you realise I almost got reported for not caring for my

kids?' I asked Lisa, holding in tears, and I immediately thought how coming clean was perhaps the worst of ideas, that the bitch could even use it against me.

Lisa said nothing.

'Do you realise what I mean?' I asked again.

'They will sort you out,' she promised.

I was mute.

'So can I put you down for the Himalayas, then?' Lisa was a driller.

By four I had already been emailed dates, preparation material and an agenda. Lisa was good. Dragon Lady would have loved to have her as her assistant. I texted my husband and told him to ignore the previous message and ask for holiday time next week; as a matter of extreme urgency. I had been enrolled in a senior programme to the Himalayas.

We were six in all from different departments and I had never met one of them.

We travelled business class from our different locations and met at a five-star lodge in Kathmandu, where I was told by a young, sleek man in black, who looked like a magician, to keep from sharing experiences with my fellow travellers because it would interfere with the programme. I would probably still know nothing about my colleagues once I left Kathmandu.

The morning after, we were all efficiently picked and packed onto another plane to Lukla, together with a plant-based chef, a nutrition expert and a motivational speaker who had not made it to the hotel the night before. (The fitness boot-camp manager and fitbox method trainer were apparently waiting for us at the Himalayan resort already.) Then onto a helicopter until we reached the limit. There, at over three thousand metres, hidden on a ridge overlooking the Everest range, was our remarkable establishment; twelve rooms only, all with stunning views. 'Should we not have been trained to live at this altitude?' My head felt like a pressure cooker.

Our week-long programme, curated by the world's authority on integrative wellness, a name that said nothing to me but then I didn't even know what integrative wellness was, would offer us access to over ten world-class practitioners in functional medicine (as opposed to dysfunctional?), yoga, Japanese Iyashi Dome and Alisselle Amethyst Quartz massage, cryotherapy and Ayurvedic treatments for dosha-balancing amongst other senseless things. It all sounded like Chinese to me and probably was. We were told the number-one objective was to teach us to cultivate equanimity.

I looked equanimity up: mental calmness and evenness of temper, especially in a difficult situation. Had Dragon Lady been to this training?

All I remember today, from the week-long tutelage that was to mend me, is the constant denial in my doctors' faces, the five different types of cat food we were fed every day, and the permanent headache from lack of oxygen, lasting from the morning-time yoga class through the long-day trek, up to the comatosing evening sessions. But also the beauty of the shrubs and rhododendron forests, I have to admit.

And I remember the last day. I remember this trek – the one I could not finish. Our master trekker kept pushing me, asking me to break it down to its simplest form, to put one foot after the other until I reached the summit. I remember thinking I was going to die on that mountain, far away from my kids, working for a company that I despised, sent on a training by a woman who I more than hated, to change me into someone I would loathe even more. At the summit, I remember our Way of Tea master held a full-blown silent tea ceremony, and we were individually helped to mimic his every move.

I had been suddenly invaded by a very strange calmness. For the first time in years, I had felt I was in control of my mind and body and could achieve serenity and happiness.

Back from the Himalayas, I called Lisa again and I resigned. This time she could not dissuade me.

My husband saw my resignation as confirmation of my breakdown rather than a wisdom of sorts and soon became estranged, convinced that a weakness had blanketed my strength and caused me to invite poverty and boredom into my life. We separated within the year. Eventually he claimed that I was mad and tried to get full custody of the kids but failed.

Since the kids started university, I have travelled the world to train as a tea master. And it was in India that I tracked down the Zen Buddhist monk who had blessed me in the Himalayas and had him teach me for five years. From India I moved to Myanmar and was next invited to join him in Japan where he was ordained in the Soto Zen tradition. When he passed away I met a man who became my second husband and together we opened Lady Dragon's Tea Hut, to teach the art of tea.

She came one day, full of nostalgia for the time when she had been beautiful and bad, odd, surprising, vexing and crude. And I told her that her Himalayan training had mended me. The tables had turned.

Life is like that; nothing funny or poetic just mocking us. Key to its survival is the art of seeing in one thing the embryo of another, like an apparition which can change you. 'I am not part of you ordinary life anymore and feel peaceful, as if those years at the bank had never counted,' I told her. I assured her that every hurt does not hurt forever.

I know she will have a good fight with death because she's still a fighter, and perhaps one day I will take to her tomb a wreath of paper daisies.

15

Teacher beggar

She thinks it's her by the cash machine buttoning up the last bit of her top; a ghost sucking a pipe in the cold, seated in stillness.
 The same long straight orange hair. The same free size boho hippie gypsy festival-type skirt; blue with sewn silver sequins all along the block prints and patches of red embroidery. She recognises this particular one as one she has seen her wear before. It has the same elastic waistband she had once told her was so practical, because it could accommodate most waist sizes, finished with cute drawstrings and tiny bells.
 She always looked old but she looks departed now, she thinks. Perhaps not older but certainly more tired, defeated by life. Her skin seems too large for what it has left to cover and hangs everywhere. Her arms are nude under a filthy shawl; she must be freezing. She is half-covering her head with a sixties fake-leather white cap, but she still knows it's her. She is almost certain.
 She is seated on the floor over a blanket watching the hordes plod by. There is no question she could not just have fallen there, or put herself there to rest for a second because she has lost her breath or her bearings. She seems to be there permanently, by the cash machine, although she could not be sure she is asking for money. She is reclining against the wall of the supermarket.

SOUR PRICKS

When a young man passes by, she hears her ask him for a cigarette. It is definitely her voice and it makes her tremble. She holds her daughter's little hand tightly and tries to hide her behind her own body: that woman two years ago had been her daughter's nursery teacher.

She feels awful about hiding her kid from the teacher but she doesn't want the teacher to see the girl, and she doesn't want to have to explain to her daughter that the world is ugly.

Once when her daughter had still been at the nursery, she had taken her to Benny's for a drink on a sunny afternoon after collection time, no more than two blocks from where they are currently standing, and the little girl had enquired about a man begging on a corner, a homeless man. She had explained to her that the man didn't have a home. Next, the girl had naturally proposed to offer him their second home to sleep in that night. She had remained speechless, finding no fitting remark quickly enough. So she had congratulated her daughter on her thinking, secretly thanking her for pouring into the world's dark skull some of her peculiar light, until the girl forgot about it once her ice cream arrived to their table. She would not be any better at explaining things to her girl now, she thinks.

Has the teacher lost her job at the nursery? She was so well-liked. But then she was getting old and had suffered from depression after her husband passed away. Poor thing! She suddenly remembers when the teacher had shared suspicions with her that the new management didn't like her, because she smelled of cigarettes; some mothers had apparently complained. But she had reassured the teacher her livelihood would be protected because she was a fixture in that nursery, a long-stander. She had been there for over forty years caring for two if not three generations of local children. Still the teacher claimed her new bosses didn't really value that, that they didn't understand that.

She recalls the teacher telling her how she had seen things change. How local people were now different, business had changed, values had changed.

The teacher hadn't liked her at first, she had confessed, when she had asked for her daughter to do only half days so the girl could spend the other half at a private nursery.

The teacher didn't believe in private education; she didn't believe in the rich having better opportunities and getting richer. She thought what she taught was as good as what those rich babies' nurseries taught, and the rich nurseries' job was all about 'defining' an elite, which was toxic to society.

She had agreed with the teacher at the time but then that was how the world worked, and she wanted the best for her child.

The light turns green and she pulls her child through the crossing, coming a step away from the cash machine, still trying to hide her girl from her teacher.

She feels terrible but she assures herself the teacher would feel embarrassed for her old pupil to see her like that. What if her daughter said something inappropriate? What if the teacher said something inappropriate? Perhaps the teacher has lost her head as well as her livelihood? Maybe the teacher has given herself to drink? Or perhaps she will jump at her child, who she loved, and hug her and the girl will be frightened! She knows all these thoughts are bad. But she's still hurrying at full speed past the cash machine, her eyes set on the floor, dragging her child behind her as quickly as she can.

'Why are you rushing me?' her daughter asks, her half-croissant about to fall from the grasp of her hand.

'Marci is waiting for us at home,' she tells her. 'Your drums teacher could be there already.' She's lying. The music teacher is not due for another half an hour.

But she's determined she will drop off her daughter and come back out. She will come back to the teacher. She cannot leave things like this. She's trying to remember her name. *What was she called? What was she called?* She cannot ask her daughter, of course. She needs to remember. Perhaps she can search amongst her papers at home.

At home, she leaves her daughter with Marci to unpack school bags, set the homework and change, and digs into the old nursery folder but finds nothing.

In the safety of her house, she starts feeling perhaps she should forget about it. What can she do? What good will it do to let the teacher know she is aware of her situation? She can perhaps give her some money, buy her some food. But she knows she cannot really help her in the longer term. She couldn't get her a job; they already have Marci. And the teacher is quite old. And the truth is she does trust her but would not particularly want her around the house. Neither would her husband. What would it change if she goes back to see her now?

She hears her child calling her.

'You said you had to go out?' the child asks.

'Yes,' she can't backtrack. 'Just for a minute.'

'Can you get some milk? Marci says there is no more milk?'

'Sure.'

'And stop at the one pound shop for a pencil sharpener. I need a new pencil sharpener,' the child orders her mother.

'You could have told me before!'

'Sorry Mum.'

'No problem, I will be back in a minute.' She has no option now.

As she's by the door with her coat on, she feels her kid's hand on her arm, dragging her back. She bends to kiss her daughter's forehead.

'I don't know why but I just keep thinking about Pamela,' her daughter whispers near her mum's ear.

Suddenly it comes to her. That was her name. Pamela. 'Pamela, who?' she says.

'You know, my old nursery teacher.'

She swallows and smiles, trying to hide her discomfort.

'Can we go visit her in the nursery one of these days?'

'Sure.' She kisses her daughter again, mortified, and leaves down the stairs.

As she approaches the cash machine she can see the teacher is still there. She's in the same position as before. Nothing has changed.

She approaches her, almost embarrassed, considering what other people may think when they see her in conversation with a beggar. There are plenty of parents from her daughter's school she often sees around these parts. What does it matter? She does not need to explain herself to anybody. And her daughter... Had she seen her teacher by the cash machine just before? Was she asking her to please go sort things out? Was this her daughter's way to fight, the only way she can at her age? If anything, she decides she has to do this for her own daughter.

'Hi Pamela, my God, how are you?' she says. She doesn't like speaking down to the teacher, so she's crouching to speak at her same level when a strong smell invades her nostrils, making it hard for her not to back away.

The woman looks straight at her. Her eyes tiny and dry, the same eyes that have consoled so many children over the years, including her own daughter. She's sure she has recognised her. She's certain. 'Who are you?' the teacher asks her.

'You know, Gemma's mum from the nursery.'

A pigeon is approaching the teacher's knee on the floor, and the teacher reaches out with her hand to caress it, which disgusts Gemma's mum.

'Which nursery?' the teacher asks.

'You know the nursery behind here in the square,' she points in the direction of the old nursery, 'the one you taught at?'

'I didn't teach at no nursery,' the teacher holds her stare and she's uncertain whether to insist or not. 'Do you have a ciggie, mam?' the teacher asks her.

She hesitates. She feels this can't finish with a ciggie. But she doesn't know how to fix something like this.

'Sure. What do you smoke? I'll buy you some,' she finally gives in.

'Anything,' the teacher says.

'Can I get you some food or drink too?' she offers, at least a small gesture.

'Can't eat much with my teeth, love.' The teacher frightens her, showing a grim machined-down wall of maroon-green teeth. 'Maybe a hot cup of tea,' the teacher adds after coughing a bad cough.

'Where are you staying tonight? It's cold,' she asks but the teacher doesn't answer.

After about five minutes, she comes back with a hot tea and a pack of Berkeley but the teacher has gone.

At bedtime, she's tucking in her daughter after their reading. 'Do you want an extra blanket? It was cold last night.'

'Yes, Mummy.'

As she comes back with the blanket, she sees her daughter kneeling on the side of the bed, her hands together. Another yoga position? It seems to be a new craze at school.

'It's going to be a cold night again, right?' her daughter asks her. 'I am praying for the homeless.'

She feels like something has crept in under cover of darkness and turned the soil. This happy girl's life is already being taken from her.

'Good girl,' she says, pulling her daughter towards her, then she lets her huddle her duvet and goes back into the living room.

She knows they're both thinking about Pamela somewhere out there in the cold.

16

FEMINISTA

I think we get a bad lot, women. I also think that we don't help ourselves. And I never wanted to wave the feminist flag but I decided it would be fun. So I made a list.

There was to be seven girls.

First Elasaid, my Turkish neighbour who had moved here recently from Athens. She used to be an architect there, before the city fell and she flew to London as a cooking-oil importing entrepreneur. She was married, two kids. Baby platinum locks falling like tiny waterfalls down the cutest, mousy face. She had perfect teeth and a sexy accent, according to the porter of our building. She always wore jeans with loose cotton blouses, preferably flowery, and canvas shoes. You could tell she had smoked a lot of pot in her youth and had only recently upgraded from AC/DC T-shirts, perhaps after hitting parenthood.

Next Jimena, the sharp corporate lawyer at a top tobacco company whose husband had worked with mine. She was a Latina explosion at every turn. Tall, voluptuous in the right way that makes men crazy. Big eyes and pleasure-seeking lips she perfectly combined with high heels, low necklines or backless dresses. She was a license-to-kill freed around the streets of London; no wonder her husband worried.

Then there was Fathima, daughter of the titan. Petite. Dark. Bejewelled. She was a type. We had met through a friend of a friend of my husband, and our kids had ended up in the same school.

Fourth, Riya. The chubby girl, called herself a *danseuse*. She claimed to be a specialist in Asian dancing but I had actually met her at a tango lesson. There was no ounce without bounce amongst all her plumpness, and her black eyes were legendary as well as her penchant for shiny clothing.

Adalene, the French girl, because no feminist club can survive without a Frenchie, was my fifth victim. She had attended hat-making lessons with me. (And I know you are probably judging me already, as the kind of woman at this or that other course all day rather than helping my husband make an honest living, which doesn't sound very feminist at all. But things are never what they seem.) Adalene was a Chanel-chic chick with a blonde bob. You could lose yourself in her huge, calm blue eyes which embezzled her husband and hypnotized her toddlers into little zombie soldiers. But her nails were those of a panther.

And one but last Priya, my teacher of Indian cuisine. She was a rebounder. The least sexy of all perhaps but the most mystical, her hair as long, dark and snaky as Medusa's. And she had just launched her own interior design business despite being a cook, together with Adelene who she too had met at the sought-after hat-making classes.

Of course the seventh girl, in case you are wondering, was me.

What did these girls have in common?

At least a vagina. And that they knew me and me them, and for one reason or another I liked them and they me at least a little. They each had plenty of attributes too for which I disliked them (and they me again), of course, but one needs to concentrate on the positives.

Once the girls had all accepted to become members of my club, *FEMINISTA*, I wrote the rules, intentionally disregarding the possibility of an ethics committee to oversee any methodology. There were to be seven rules for seven girls:
1. I would send a sexy location once a month by WhatsApp, strictly five stars. Always a Saturday evening.
2. Everyone was expected to drink and at least a third of us would smoke. No mobile devices were allowed.
3. Sexy knickers and/or stockings were compulsory; we had a choice. No other dress code. Except Jimena was not allowed to wear her trademark heels; she was the tallest by far and it just got embarrassing.
4. Kids or talk of kids was strictly prohibited as motherhood is as overrated as the Christian trinity.
5. Work-talk was only allowed if it went somewhere saucy. If it didn't, we had to make it by faking it. We didn't need to own up to what was true versus what was fiction – a relief.
6. We would always look at men openly and discuss their merits loudly.
7. We each brought a poem, four lines, to play recite-roulette round the table. The poem had to be about sex, but unlike the rest of the evening, it had to talk real.

Our first date was at Zuma, behind a building facing Harrods. Despite being hidden, everybody knew it. The private room holds fifteen, which in London means seven comfortably, and the intricate wood paneling allows you to peek into the principal party scene of the main restaurant, a must to comply with *FEMINISTA*'s rule six, though we could always have dinner in peace and hit Zuma's famous bar later, in search of the Arab princes with violet neon Lamborghinis parked outside. You bet!

I had arranged the menu in advance, the cheaper of two options.

On the day.

The first incoming tray of drinks had a rubabu, rhubarb-infused Daiginjo sake with wild strawberry liqueur; three Zuma Bellinis, ripe apricots stirred shaken with Cape North vodka and fresh passion fruit, Wokki sake and Billecart-Salmon champagne; two zumanuka, fresh basil muddled with 42 Below manuka honey vodka, juicy pineapple and a dash of Jonagold apple juice; and a fig-Manhattan, one-month aged in an old-fashioned sherry cask, with the slightest hint of Campari.

'Are you kidding me? I had never heard of an "aged" cocktail!' someone yelled around the table, impressed.

We mingled over our drinks for twenty minutes, talking property values going up, blood pressures down, garden geraniums, the state of the financial system and antique parchment paper for treasure maps. Enough to be thirsty for more.

After a repeat round, same cocktails exactly as we weren't stupid enough to beg for a headache the next day, we showed each other our underwear. (I told you women don't help themselves!)

Fathima wore strip-club fuschia and black with a brassy edge, great with her skin colour; Adalene was in a white lace corset-y instrument with matching stockings like gorgeous Bey in the video for her last single; Elsaid flashed a Perry-styled pretty pink balcony bra and briefs; Jimena stripped sensually behind the table so we could admire her take on Pam Anderson: a shiny satin, dark-ocean-blue combo teamed with skyscraper heels overruling her heels restriction on some petty yet tight legal argument – she was a top lawyer! A polka dot set with Wonderbra elaborate garters and suspender belts from Riya, great choice; and a Bardot meets Matalan babydoll black combo from Priya, who looked a bit like a bored housewife. And of course my own, black superU briefs, no bra. We were doing well up to rule five.

Elasaid had brought some pot too to take care of the smoking; it was first class. A wholesaler gifted it to her, all the way from Morocco, she told us.

'Is that on the way to Greece?' someone joked. 'Does he hide it inside your cooking oil?'

The Spanish waiter had a good nose and got a whiff of the weed straight away but let us off. He only asked if anyone had any phoney dietary restrictions and was startled when we didn't.

During our starters to share, piri kara dofu salad fried tofu with avocado and japanese herbs, maguro no sashimi sliced seared tuna with soy ginger lime and coriander, gyu no tataki seared beef with chilli daikon and ponzu sauce, suzuki (not the motorbike) thinly sliced sea bass with green chilli and lime, and ika no kari kari age crispy fried squid with yuzu truffle oil and salmon roe, Riya started us on the work front.

She talked reforms to soldiers' housing. We thought, 'Soldiers, box ticked!' It definitely made us feel bubbly, like we were going somewhere. Riya really impressed us. She was not only an Asian *danseuse* and a tango aficionado but held a top job at the MOD! Who would have thought it! Or perhaps she was making it up, but then that was allowed under club rules.

Elisaid discussed the good looks of some of her Greek saucisson pieces imported with the oil. We giggled.

Jimena instead chatted about her affair with a top dog, the highest biller in her firm focusing on environmental law and toxic tort cases. 'Don't you work in a tobacco corporate?' someone attempted to clarify. Prior to establishing his own practice, Jimena's lover had served as law clerk for the Chief United States District Judge for the District of Montana. He was hot – she showed us a picture of him in padded cycling pants.

Fathima was also having an affair, allegedly, with her husband's boss. This was the nearest to job talk from her but then her father was a titan and she didn't need to work. We mostly all thought her affair was a fib; I could see it in the girls faces. Adelena had joined a new class after the hat-making experience, in nude painting. She insisted courses were part of her career and further education, because bettering herself was what she was paid for by her husband and it occupied all her time free of her children. She had got friendly with her new painting instructor and asked for 'extra', following which he had taught her how to make a nude man come just by looking at him. We begged for her to teach us.

Priya had been busy too in her new guise as top interior designer and decorator; she had just sketched the perfect sofa to make love on... We were so curious but she insisted we would have to wait for the big launch.

And finally me: I talked about my work setting up *FEMINISTA*, and promised our next meeting would include a surprise guest. Everyone cheered. 'Will there be a pole?' someone yelled around the table.

We asked for another round of drinks, same exactly, as we weren't stupid enough to beg for a headache the next day, as I said.

After our mains, to share, ainame no koumi yaki to kousou grilled Chilean sea bass (that fish again), tsubu-miso gako hinadori no oven yaki barley, miso marinated baby chicken oven-roasted on cedar wood, karei no kara age crispy fried sole with green chilli ginger dressing and garlic hojiso butter, ise ebi fuumi, and roasted lobster with spicy ponzu sauce and green onions, we peeked through the ornate gates of our enclosure in search of men in the open sea.

They were all a bit plodgy. Old. Quite rich, probably. Mostly taken. No devil-may-care subaltern gigolos. Many were definitely gay, and at least one looked like a transvestite, from Warhol's factory. We got a bit depressed, concluded our best bets were the waiters. But we would not let it get to us and planned to join the bar later.

Only some of us had space for dessert, and the nerves were rising ahead of our poetry recital.

We were iron ladies but hardly wrote poems. We hardly recited poems. We almost never talked about sex in detail and we hardly ever told the truth. The time had come to do all four of these things, simultaneously, and the prospect seemed worse than dehorning a goat; it was nerve-wracking. We took the cute name cards I had designed for the table with the *FEMINISTA* logo, and let them get lost in the depth of Jimena's stocking. 'How many men would have paid to be those name cards!'

Priya took the first name out. It was Fathima. She gulped her Bellini; she had written her poem on rose-scented paper.

tv off, tesoro! don't I look divine?
let's melt together, it may turn all fine
feel me in your hands, cover me with dew
let's make it one, to shine amongst the few

Riya applauded. Jimena looked suspicious. Priya put her hand to her mouth and lowered her eyelids as if burdened with lust. Elisaid's eyes were moist. Adalene frowned. I was a stone.

Priya took the second name out. It was Elisaid; her poem was written softly with pencil on cigarette rolling paper.

> *I promised you beauty, I promised to inspire*
> *I guess you dreamed else than having me on fire*
> *don't fret, don't freeze, don't sigh, don't scowl*
> *I need to feel you! before I re-gown*

Riya applauded. Jimena looked more suspicious than before. Priya put both hands to her mouth and winked mischievously. Fathima shed a tear. Adalene double-frowned. I was a stone.

We all took a spoon in turns of Riya's green tea and banana cake, which the Spanish waiter had brought in full of smiles, with seven spoons.

Priya took the next name out of the stocking: Adelene. Her poem was black ink on red paper; she had rolled it into a tube worn in her garter.

> *I whip you, I slash you until you turn red*
> *this is the way, how you like it in bed*
> *to soothe your pains you look into my eyes*
> *but you never want any close to my thighs*

Riya applauded. Did she understand English at all? Jimena looked the most suspicious we had ever seen her, yet, almost enough to wish she was a women lawyer rather than slaving at a tobacco company. Priya put her hands to her eyes as if to hide her shame. Elasaid laughed then stopped herself. Fathima started crying; tears did not come out but we all knew she was crying. I was a stone.

We asked for another round of drinks, same drinks exactly to all the other rounds we had lost count of, as we weren't stupid enough to beg for a headache the next day, you all know. The Spanish waiter congratulated us on our drinking but must have noticed the change in mood... Some of the girls already looked like they were building a grudge against *FEMINISTA*, promising to themselves never again they should be tempted to donate believing they could avoid being enlisted.

Priya took Riya's name out of the stocking next, as she was still savouring the last bit of her cake. She had not written down her poem; she claimed she knew it my heart.

God has given you a dirty digit
should have married you to someone frigid
you want to live up there, close to my dung
your way to love feels like a pang

Jimena looked furious. Priya hid under the table. Elisaid laughed then stopped herself, gulped her rubabu all in one. Adalene was frowning again. Fathima looked like an airtight pot about to explode. I was a stone.

Then Priya took her own name out of the stocking, stood up and revealed her poem hidden in the depths of a beautiful shiny cream shell she had carried buried in her snake dark hair.

you prefer its touch to my skin
claiming it gives you a sheen
petrol, honey, shower of gold
what you ask of me leaves me cold

Once Priya finished reading, Fathima stood up and walked out in the direction of the ladies', rivers down her face. Jimena followed her speedily in her heels; we heard her say something under her breath about enough material for a class-action; we were certainly full of *bon mots* and *apercus* for our husbands.

Priya sat back down and leaned her head up to admire the elaborate artwork on the ceiling. Her shell that she had left on the table rolled and fell to the floor.

Elisaid kept giggling, and we had realised by then it was the effect of the pot. Adalene said, 'Fuck it,' and took her mobile out of her tiny Gucci bag to check her messages, in contravention of club rules.

Riya got up and started dancing on her own around the table, then felt momentarily stupid and left to the ladies' to join Priya and Jimena. After ten minutes, they had not come back.

Priya threw a look at Adalene and lit a cigarette. They were both bored.

Elisaid kept giggling lost in space.
I got up, paid the bill with the club's funds and eloped silently.
FEMINISTA never again.

Made in the USA
Columbia, SC
23 February 2019